The Uzi swung his way

It was a hard-edged shadow that barely separated from the surrounding darkness. Barrabas dropped like a puppet that has just had its strings cut. It was sheer reflex that made him dig his heels in and push off at the same moment, simultaneous action prompted by the imminent threat that promised to bring death in the night.

Even as he toppled, he managed to complete the instinctive motion of his hand and drew his weapon. A stream of projectiles tore by him, and as he hit the ground he rolled, the Browning Hi-Power angled toward the looming dark shape.

There was no time left. One shot was all the chance he had.

He squeezed the trigger.

SOLDIERS OF BARRABAS

SOLDIERS OF BARRABAS

THE BARRABAS THRUST

JACK HILD

A GOLD EAGLE BOOK FROM
WORLDWIDE®

TORONTO • NEW YORK • LONDON • PARIS
AMSTERDAM • STOCKHOLM • HAMBURG
ATHENS • MILAN • TOKYO • SYDNEY

First edition July 1989

ISBN 0-373-61631-7

Special thanks and acknowledgment to
Rich Rainey for his contribution to this work.

1

London, Late August

Thomas Crowell burst into his Covent Garden flat at two in the morning, leaving his keys jangling in the lock as he raced for the ringing phone.

He'd just spent ten exhausting hours assembling footage for *Arms Bizarre*, his BBC documentary on the shadowy world of arms dealers. But he sprinted down the hallway just the same, snatching the phone to his ear and shouting, "Hello!"

He was like most people who trafficked in privileged information: his life was largely governed by late-night callers, many of them anonymous.

"Crowell?"

The electronically altered voice took him by surprise. At another time it might have amused him, but at two in the morning the robotic voice had a sinister edge.

"Yes," Crowell said. "Who's this?"

"The proverbial friend of a friend."

"Aren't they all," Crowell said. "Would your friend be Frankenstein, perhaps?" He was irritated with the caller, wondering if it was a simple prankster or one of his legion of enemies. "What's this about?"

"Stolen weapons from an American air base."

Whoever the man was, he knew what Crowell was after. He proceeded to tip him about an arms transfer the next evening, then hung up before Crowell could question him further, leaving a hollow silence behind.

Crowell reluctantly cradled the phone. Until that very moment he'd considered his three-part documentary almost complete. But now it looked like it was really just starting.

The documentary featured silhouette interviews with Crowell's usual intelligence contacts and dramatic reenactments of murders connected to the weapons trade. But it was still missing something.

Arms Bizarre lacked actual footage of a weapons deal taking place, the kind of high-power visuals that made documentaries come to life.

Since the caller had sounded legit, perhaps that flaw could be remedied, he mused.

The following night Thomas Crowell drove his film crew in a surveillance van down past Richmond Park, the medieval forest preserve that drew Londoners from the muggy confines of the capital on heat-drenched nights. They came via underground station or made the short drive by car, then walked through the park or soaked up a few beers at one of the inns that overlooked the Thames.

Lately the park was full of long-haired hitchhikers with khaki packs and bedrolls who stayed hidden in the park long after the gates were locked. Most of them were young kids who trekked from city to city in the wake of their favorite band's concerts.

At 9:15 Crowell's van crunched into the graveled lot of Church Grim's Inn, just outside the town of Richmond. He backed the van into a corner of the lot tucked under the shadows of tall whispering oaks.

He glanced first at Doreen Lowndes, the auburn-haired woman riding shotgun, then back at Roger Carmichael, the cameraman who shepherded equipment in the back of the van.

"Okay, lady and gentleman," Crowell said. "Let's roll 'em."

In a few moments his crew set up the long-range night-vision TV cameras to scan the entire lot through the van's bubble windows. Crowell turned on the split-screen monitor mounted waist-high in the wall of the van.

Now came the hard part. The waiting.

According to Crowell's informant, the meeting was set for 10:30, so there was plenty of time before the dealers arrived. But just to be on the safe side—in case one of the parties was already there and had noticed the dark green van with tinted windows—Crowell took Doreen inside the Inn for a quick drink and a bite.

They returned within a half hour to find Roger stoically manning the cameras.

"Anything?" Crowell said.

"No," Roger said, "except for a couple of buggers who went to hoist a few and didn't bring me back round one."

"Sorry," Crowell said, patting his stomach. "But we had to make it look good."

"Next time you gotta make it look good, take me," Roger said.

"You're not as pretty as she is," Crowell said, drawing a smile from Doreen as she manned her post.

They fell into the quiet trancelike state that always enveloped them on long surveillance assignments. Occasionally Crowell rested his head against the soft upholstered wall of the van, closing his eyes to permit a few precious moments of half sleep.

But he had to stay awake. He passed the time looking at the scenery, outside the van as well as in.

Doreen was definitely worth looking at. Her long auburn hair tumbled down her shoulders in natural corkscrew curls that reminded him of the girls he used to know back in the sixties.

She was just a few years out of university and already was shooting up through the ranks, proving once again that talent and beauty were a potent mix.

The one aggravating thing about her was the way she looked on her present assignments as simple tasks and petty annoyances, little more than signposts on the way to her real job at the top.

Crowell had been slogging it out for nearly twenty years and was only now getting places, earning a reputation that was starting to open up doors. He'd smartened up a bit over the years and finally learned how to play politics.

In the old days he would have given her a hard time on the way up, maybe throwing a roadblock or two in her way. But he had come to realize the grand scheme of things. In a few years he just might have to tug at her skirt for the plum assignments she'd be handing out from on high.

At intervals headlights splayed over the surveillance van, boosting his adrenaline, but each time it was a false alarm. Just regular patrons of the inn.

Although a few more couples left the inn, riding away in cars parked near the van, the lot stayed fairly full, enough so Crowell didn't worry about the van sticking out.

Forty minutes passed with no sign of the vehicles Crowell's informant had mentioned. They grew edgy, and once again they went over the plans. If anyone suspicious approached the van to peer in the dark windows, Crowell and Doreen would hurry up front and make like passionate lovers. Not a bad deal, Crowell thought, almost hoping it would happen.

If things got out of hand and their cover was blown, or if they were in any danger, Crowell would act as the wheelman and drive them the hell out of there.

There were a half dozen other contingencies they had agreed upon, such as how long they'd wait if the deal didn't go down on time, and how far they'd follow if the weapons deal moved elsewhere.

Finally, when they were all thinking that Crowell had been had, it happened. Quickly and casually.

A white Volkswagen bus pulled into the lot and parked almost opposite the surveillance van.

Doreen and Roger focused the television cameras on them.

"Okay, we got two guys in the Volkswagen," Roger said.

"Short hair in military cuts," Doreen said.

"Good," Crowell said. "That ties in with what our caller said about flyboys. Looks like he's playing straight with us."

A gray station wagon entered the lot, circled the gravel boundaries once, then drove over and parked next to the Volkswagen.

"Let me have a look," Crowell said, easing Doreen away from the image intensification tube, tracking the station wagon in the green cat's-eye scope. These were the guys he was interested in.

The way Crowell's informant laid it out, U.S. airmen were steadily supplying stolen submachine guns and .45 pistols along with occasional bonuses like packets of C-4 explosive. In exchange they received top dollar, or if they wanted, they could get their currency in cocaine.

The buyers were Crowell's real targets. They were the ones who made it all happen.

Another car hurried into the parking lot. Crowell kept his eye on it until it wheeled around and parked out of sight. He heard a girlish voice laughing, her voice fading as she and her escort stepped toward the entrance of the inn.

Two men got out of the back seat of the gray station wagon. The second man carried a canvas satchel.

"What the hell?" Crowell said, tracking the first man who'd stepped out of the car and started to walk toward the Volkswagen. He looked vaguely familiar.

He had a narrow axlike face with a widow's peak of dark hair honed to a short, sharp dagger tip on his forehead.

The man looked directly into Crowell's eyes, right down the lens, almost as if he knew he was being filmed. The chilling gaze kicked up the pace of his heartbeat. But then the man scanned the rest of the parking lot with the same steady gaze, keeping his hands in the pockets of his denim jacket all the time.

I know I've seen him before, Crowell thought. "Damn it!"

"What is it?" Roger said.

"I know the first guy," Crowell said. "I think. But I don't know from where." It must have been years since he'd seen the man. But the conviction came to Crowell that they had even talked. He could almost hear the man's voice, almost match it to that predator's face. A detective working undercover? That was it, Crowell thought. He'd certainly run into his share of detectives. "Probably the police," he said.

"That explains it!" Doreen crowed. "They gave us the tip—"

"So we could film them in action," Crowell finished.

"Wouldn't be the first time they wanted a bit of glory on the telly," Roger said.

"Uh-huh," Crowell said, thinking that it would all make sense if only he had the time. "Okay," he said, handing control of the camera back to Doreen, glancing at the monitor when the two men climbed into the back seat of the Volkswagen. "Keep it on the guy in the back seat of the bus if you can."

He looked over at Roger and said, "Give me exterior shots of the vehicles. Hold the license numbers for five seconds, then pan the lot before coming back to the station wagon. Then zoom in on the driver."

Crowell looked at Doreen and said, "Track whatever comes out of the Volkswagen when they make the transfer."

"Holy shit!" Roger shouted. "Something's wrong. Look at the driver—"

"Oh God," Doreen screamed.

Crowell snapped his gaze back to the monitor.

The driver of the Volkswagen was craning his neck forward, unnaturally so. He started waving his hands, then his head jerked suddenly. He dropped down onto the wheel, revealing the ax-faced man in the back seat holding a long-barreled automatic.

"He fucking killed him!" Roger said. "He's no cop—"

Before their horrified eyes, and without further ado, the man in the front passenger seat met the same fate, his head recoiling from a bullet to the temple.

"Get us out of here!" Doreen shrieked.

Crowell was already darting for the front of the van when, with a prying metallic sound, the driver's door popped open.

A spiked-haired man lunged into the van, gun barrel first. Crowell backed away as the intruder balanced himself on the steering wheel. He waved the silenced weapon on the film crew like a scolding finger. "Don't move, gents," he said.

Roger sank against the wall, nodding his head.

It was going to be all right, Crowell thought, as long as they did what they were told.

But then Doreen moved. She hurtled by Roger, stepping on him in her fear as she dived for the back door. She crashed into it, managed to lever it open, then threw herself out onto the lot, landing knee first on the gravel. She cried from the pain as she scrambled to her feet.

Her cry was followed by muted, coughing sounds. *Phyyt. Phyyt.* The crying stopped.

Two men who had emerged out of the night threw her into the van, the back of her head disintegrating, her hair flying wildly like a bloody-tendriled Medusa. She dropped like soft stone to the floor.

The man who'd killed Doreen aimed his silenced automatic at Roger's head. Then the ax-faced man appeared in the open door, his approach masked by the shadows. "No!" he said. "Don't kill him."

The assassin shrugged and lowered the silencer toward Roger's knee.

"Not that, either," the man said, climbing into the back of the van. He looked once at Crowell and said, "We meet again."

Crowell couldn't talk. His heart, throat and tongue had all melted into one quivering panicked organ. He had become six feet of shaky, lead-footed fear.

The man's name came to Crowell's mind, if not his lips. Derek Martin. It didn't make sense. But then again, neither did dying. Crowell didn't make a move.

"Scope 'em," Derek said.

One of the assassins cut Roger's shirt from shoulder to forearm, then another man deftly plunged a hypodermic needle into the crook of his elbow.

They moved on to Crowell, cutting his shirt like netherworld medics. He sat there immobile, a robot thankfully bereft of thought as they plunged a needle into his arm.

And all the while Derek Martin stood at the back of the van admiring its high-tech contents.

Scope 'em, he'd said. They were using scopolamine, Crowell realized. The wrong mix could kill. Curiously, though, as the drug started to work on him, Crowell found himself thinking there was nothing to worry about. These guys knew what they were doing.

As he faded away he looked up at Derek Martin, who seemed to be enjoying the tableau he'd created.

Derek Martin made films, Crowell thought, dimly remembering interviewing him about a rabid political film he'd made several years back. He was only a goddamn movie director.

But the men he was directing tonight sure as hell weren't actors.

CROWELL SLOWLY FLOATED to consciousness, struggling with a dense pillowy sensation that seemed to massage his brain. He was sitting at a table in a stark white room, the walls soundproofed with baffled tiles.

Bright fluorescent strips of light hummed from the ceiling, hurting his eyes when he looked up. Crowell cautiously stretched his feet and arms, then gingerly moved his head to take a look around the room.

He noted a security camera that watched him from a berth in a corner.

Groggily he stood and headed for the door, feeling like a doped-up rodent in a laboratory test. It was locked. He went back to the table, noticing the camera track his movements.

"Where am I?" he shouted. "Where's Roger?" He glared at the mute camera before collapsing back into the plain wooden chair. He leaned over the table like a drunkard and waited.

About five minutes later Derek Martin stepped into the room, clean shaven and looking perfectly rested. He didn't look anything like a killer. In fact, he looked every bit the successful director that he was.

"So," Derek said. "Now we can talk." He pulled out a chair and sat across from Crowell.

Crowell nodded. The last time he'd spoken with Derek Martin was for a TV magazine show about angry young filmmakers who were going to change the face of cinema. That was nearly twenty years ago at the start of both of their careers.

Cinema hadn't changed much since then, but Martin's career had. He'd metamorphosed from a violence-prone director of left-wing flicks into a bankable creator of solid exploitation films.

But apparently he had never abandoned his real politics. He'd just taken them underground, although most people who remembered the reclusive director thought he'd just become one more sellout.

"Surprised?" Martin asked.

"Of course," Crowell said, grateful for the chance to establish rapport with his captor—and avoid discussing the reason they were meeting again. "You wanted to tear down the walls last time we talked. Turn society on its head."

"Still do," Martin said, talking with Crowell in the manner of a professional colleague. "I thought I could do it with my films," he said. "When I realized it was impossible—back then—I channeled my energies in different directions. As you've seen."

"It was an anonymous tip," Crowell volunteered.

Martin dismissed the subject with a wave of his hand. "Don't worry about that. I'm not going to torture you to reveal your sources. That only happens in movies. The way it works in real life is that you and I will negotiate a deal. Then you'll tell me anything I ask because it will be in your interest to."

"What do you want from me?" Crowell asked.

"As I said, in the old days it was impossible to influence world affairs with simple films. But these days, with the right kind of people working for me, the right kind of film could . . . change a lot of people."

Crowell kept up the pretense that they were professionals merely discussing a project.

"What kind of film?"

"A documentary," Martin said. "Sort of. Like the type you make. I have some backers in the media who can help my work. You can be one of them."

His lips stretched into a dagger-thin smile. The negotiations had begun.

"And if I don't want to . . ." Crowell said.

"Then you feed eels at the bottom of the Thames."

"What if I say yes?"

"It's not that simple," Martin said. "You have to demonstrate good faith with us."

"How do I do that?"

The director reached inside his denim jacket and pulled out a pocket gun, a Smith & Wesson 61 Escort. He slid the .22 LR automatic to the center of the wooden table. Then he sat back, idly slipping his hands into his pockets.

"It's only got one round," Martin said. "That's for your pal, Roger."

Crowell stared at the automatic. "He's all right?"

"For now," Martin said. "But he's got a very short life expectancy. Saw too much. Knows too much."

"Where is he?"

"Right next door in a room like this. Sitting there scared to death, wondering when it's going to happen. Come on then, let's get it over with."

Waves of nausea swept through Crowell's body, making him lean forward and hunch miserably over the table. The pistol looked bigger, gleaming like the coils of a poisonous snake. He hadn't touched a weapon since his war correspondent days.

"I can't—"

Derek shrugged. "It's your only way out."

"But why..."

The director shook his head. "Insurance. You'll never be able to prove anything about me, but possibly you might still try. So if you're going to work with me, I have to make sure you don't even think of going to the law. If you do this hit on film, I can trust you."

"I've worked with Roger for years now. I can't just go in there and...and kill him."

"It's not as hard as you think," Martin said, rocking back and forth on his chair.

Crowell stared at him, looking for signs of a madman. But instead he saw only a man who appeared to be truly in his element. "How can we explain it?" he protested. "I can't just walk away from here and say I got the jump on you all, now can I?"

"Don't worry about that," Martin said. "It will look realistic. After all, that's my trademark. You'll have to sustain some injuries before we let you out of here. If you get to that point, that is."

Crowell was lost, but saw there was no way out.

"Look," Martin coaxed him. "Maybe it will help if you think of it as a cause. Everybody's got a cause. Right now I'd guess the biggest cause you got going is your life."

Crowell smacked his hand on the table. *"No! I won't do it!"*

Martin looked at him as if he were a hopeless student who'd just shown the worst possible technique.

"Maybe I'll offer him the same deal, let him shoot you before *he* gets nailed. What do you think? Think good old Roger there would turn down a deal like that?"

Martin looked on with interest as Crowell weighed the words in apparent shock. Then he reached for the gun, but his hand stopped halfway.

"Pick it up!"

He pulled the automatic toward him but still didn't pick it up.

Martin leaned forward. "Use it on Roger," he said. "Or use it on yourself." He smiled encouragingly. "You can even try it on me. Be a real hero." He lifted his arms and spread them wide, appearing totally defenseless.

But Crowell couldn't ever hope to beat a man like this, a man who choreographed every step of his life.

Martin smiled, then shoved his chair back from the table. He was almost at the door when he turned his head over his shoulder and said, "You've got thirty seconds to decide."

The door closed behind him.

Crowell picked up the gun.

2

The Crowell Crusade was the number one show ever syndicated by International News Service. Little more than a year after his escape from the gunrunners who murdered his colleagues, Thomas Crowell was as well-known in the U.S. as he was in the U.K.

His biweekly show exposed corruption around the globe, uncovering intelligence, political and financial scandals that would have otherwise been swept under the rug.

Initially INS capitalized on the celebrity of their latest recruit to boost their ratings. But his credentials as reporter, producer and war correspondent soon canonized him in the eyes of the public.

The crusader of the airwaves could do no wrong, going from victory to victory—almost as if his career were being guided by unseen hands.

THE FACE of the INS building on Fleet Street was as dark as the starless November night that shrouded London. Tinted windows shielded INS staffers from public view while they went about their business of spying on the world.

"The Black Tower," as it was called by its critics, beamed scandal and exposé twenty-four hours a day to video and tabloid subscribers around the world.

A few minutes before midnight, Thomas Crowell sat alone in his office on the top floor of the tower. It was dimly lighted, almost like a shrine, with the omnipotent eyes of a video monitor bathing him in the radiance of the current INS broadcast. The audio was low, giving the urgent but hushed tone of the newscaster a curiously tranquil effect.

Beneath the long L-shaped work station were stacks of video decks in two-inch, one-inch and three-quarter-inch format so news footage could be viewed no matter what country it came from. A snake pit of cables connected them to other recorders and monitors.

Thomas Crowell was plugged into his cocoon for the night, editing footage for his next show. He sipped from a Styrofoam cup of tepid coffee, frowned at the taste of it, then set it down next to another half-empty cup.

The phone rang just as he keystroked commands to his computer to memorize any test edits he made with the footage.

He picked up on the first ring. It was Cynthia Lane, an assistant producer who kept the same late hours as he did and made sure he knew about it.

"There's a woman on line four," she intoned, "who wants to talk to you and *only you*."

"Yeah?"

"It's a matter of life and death."

He laughed. "Isn't it always?"

"I think this one is legit," Cynthia said.

"You willing to sign that in blood?"

She paused for a moment. One of her tasks was to screen for callers who claimed that Venusians had implanted electrodes in their heads in preparation for a takeover of Earth. "She's hysterical," she summed up, "but not crazy."

"Okay," Crowell said. "Hang up when I come on." He turned on the tape recorder attached to the phone, then picked up line four. "Crowell here."

"You've got to help me—"

The voice was young. Twenties. Half-shrieking. For a moment he thought Cynthia had made a mistake and a loon got through. "Take it easy," he said soothingly. "I'll help if I can. But please, slow down."

She exhaled loudly and said, "I will."

"Why did you call?"

"I can't take it anymore—" there was a catch in her voice "—I just can't."

Crowell recognized the real wounds in her voice. Whatever the cause, the woman was in trouble. And her voice sounded vaguely familiar.

"What's your name, dear?"

"I can't tell you yet," she said, panic creeping back into her voice.

"That's no problem," he said, using his father confessor voice. "Just give me a name I can call you now."

"Okay," she complied. "G-G-Gloria."

"That's good, Gloria. Now, what can't you take anymore?"

"It's the people I'm with and the things I've done. Things they've made me do."

"What kind of people?" he asked.

"They've . . . they've killed . . . they have it on tape. Oh God, it's so horrible . . ."

"Why are you calling me?"

"Others are going to be killed . . ."

"I meant, why haven't you gone to the police?"

"Police can't stop them!" she said in an intense, scolding whisper, as though she were berating him. "You know that yourself. They've even got police working with them. Special Branch, I think. These people are assassins, dealing in political murder and blackmail."

"Who are they?" Crowell demanded. "Do they have a name?"

"Shock Troupe," she said. "It's a terrorist group with hooks into a lot of people. The leader is posing as a director. His name is Derek Martin."

"That's insane." Crowell's voice suddenly matched the urgency of his caller's. "He is a director . . . a respected man."

She sobbed before going on. "I thought he was just a filmmaker when I first met him, but he's more. He's done awful things. Murderous things. It makes me sick to think of it."

"We've got to meet," Crowell said.

"It's hard," she protested. "They watch me all the time. I shouldn't even be making this call, but we're at a different house and I don't think the phone is bugged."

"Can you leave there tonight?"

"No. I was dropped off here for someone. He's sleeping now but there's a man watching things downstairs. Maybe in a couple of days . . . I can come down there?"

"Of course!" Crowell said. "I'll set things up for you. I'll be waiting at the front door if I have to. But what about the meantime? Will you try intelligence?"

"Shock Troupe is full of their type," she said. "They're all bloody spooks!"

"I see," Crowell said, trying to keep her from hanging up. "And this Shock Troupe is planning to kill someone?"

"Yes."

"Where? Here in London?"

"London and all over."

"Okay," Crowell said. "But where is this fellow Martin staying right now?"

"King's Glen," she said. "He's got a place in King's Glen. I've got to go now! I'm too scared to stay on the line. I'll call back . . ."

"You've done the right thing, Gloria," he said.

"Thanks—" The line went dead.

Crowell put down the phone and rewound the cassette. He made a duplicate of the tape, listened to it one more time, dropped it into an envelope and sealed it.

Then he made a call. "I need a courier for a small package," he said. "Right away. It's urgent."

He locked the master tape in his safe, closed his office and took the elevator down to the lobby.

Crowell plunged into the November gloom. The wind seemed to swirl him along the street, tugging at his coat. Cold as ice, the gale numbed his fingers and made him hurry even more than he would have ordinarily.

The black car was already waiting for him at the corner. Crowell opened the passenger door and handed the envelope to a silent courier. "Don't waste time with this," he said. "Take it straight to the top. No one else looks at it. Got it?"

The man nodded without saying a word. Crowell backed out of the warm cocoon of the car and slammed the door, watching it drive into the London night. His part was done.

He washed his hands of it and went back to work.

GABRIELLA FUCSHIN was a lush-figured Valkyrie, a blond battle maiden for Shock Troupe, Derek Martin's terrorist ensemble. Derek had molded her into the kind of woman that men wished for in their dreams.

Her first name really was Gabriella. But *Fucshin*, German for vixen, was the name Derek selected for her when he plucked her from London's army of unemployed actresses.

He quickly groomed her to play much more important roles off camera, and at first she played them beautifully. She became a trusted member of the troupe, learning how to entrap the powerful men Derek sent her. The mistress became the master, conquering all, leaving them to sleep in the costly bed she'd made for them.

Bit by bit Gabriella learned more about the inner workings of the group. It turned out to be more than she wanted to know. Derek Martin was taking her places where she didn't want to go.

Now the soft-sculpted Venus was cracking, the sculptor's glaze peeling and showing the brittleness beneath. Setting up politicians and prominent businessmen for blackmail was one thing. That was the natural scheme of things. But she had come to understand that Derek's setup included murder.

That was why she'd called Thomas Crowell the previous night, using the name Gloria when he insisted on a name. Crowell had become almost a saint to her. He was the only person in the world she could really turn to, and she again invited his presence to help normalize her world.

It was ten at night, and she sat on her bed, curling her arms around her ankles as she watched the small television on her dresser.

A faithful watcher of INS, Gabriella was a believer. She felt safe when the glow of an INS report bathed her in the comfort of her bedroom.

The bedroom was on the third floor of Derek's King's Glen retreat. A retreat for everyone but her.

WRAITHS OF FLAME CRACKLED in the ember-scorched well of the nineteenth-century steel fireplace. The reflections shimmered across the gleaming Gothic pillars set into the weathered brick chimney.

Derek Martin sat in a red leather wing chair. He stared thoughtfully into the play of the flames, occasionally stroking his chin absentmindedly.

Initially he'd had a full weekend planned at the King's Glen retreat. Just an hour and a half south of London, it was the perfect place for his guests to escape the pressures of the world they helped govern.

But he'd begged off for the upcoming weekend. Things had interfered, he'd explained, and his guests understood that sometimes it was best not to be seen at the estate and took no offense at being so suddenly uninvited.

He was sipping brandy, in the manner of a country lord enjoying the fruits of his manor. Twenty years ago he would have jeered at what he'd considered a decadent self-indulgent picture. But twenty years before Derek Martin didn't own an estate; nor did he own luxury flats in London and Paris. Back then, Derek Martin was one of the angry young men of the cinema. Shock theater, underground Grand Guignol, cinema verité, he went through all of those stages.

Then his radical attitude vanished. He started to make more popular pictures. His company grew, and exploitation flicks were in the natural order of things.

Derek Martin, the leather-jacketed angry young man was mostly forgotten. The world at large knew only the Derek Martin who'd made *Rock Apocalypse*, a high school horror show that was breaking records around the world.

His past had become history. Dead. If anyone ever thought of his violent past, it was quickly glossed over. It was chalked up to being young and sowing wild oats, like joining the Communist party or soaking up a bit too much acid.

Derek Martin had become an established man in respectable society. Politicians came to him and bankers and barristers. He was a deal maker in more than just the world of the cinema.

Derek swirled the last of the brandy around in the snifter as he watched its little whirlpool with fascination.

The wind howled outside the manor, hissing against the windows almost on cue, almost like sound effects for one of the horror films they shot on location at the manor.

The country house had served as a convalescent home for American GIs during the years after World War II. It had passed through several hands, getting more expensive each time until it was bought by Derek Martin. It served as the official headquarters for his films—and the unofficial headquarters for Shock Troupe.

He walked to the desk in the middle of the room, pressed the *Rewind* button on the cassette deck and once again listened to the tape Crowell had sent the previous night.

Gabriella's taped voice shrieked out at him. "You've got to help me—"

He turned down the volume and listened as she identified herself as Gloria. It was crafty of Crowell to get her to make up a name. Most people giving a false name automatically chose a name that began with the same letter as their real name.

And Gabriella aka Gloria, had been no different.

Derek listened as she spoke about Shock Troupe and the assassination plans she'd overheard.

He shook his head, ran his hand through his hair. It fell softly, perfectly back into place.

Too bad, he thought. Just when she was coming along. She'd grown from the minor assignments and was going to be a full-fledged member of the crew.

He felt sad, not for her, but for all the work he'd put into her.

He'd expected her to betray him sooner or later, or sell out. Just like he'd scripted her life from the moment he met her. But it wasn't supposed to happen so soon. Gabriella cracked too early.

Where did he go wrong?

Still, there was always someone else in the wings. He headed down the hall, then went upstairs to tell Gabriella that her script had been changed.

Derek stopped at a room two doors away from Gabriella's. He opened the door, then grinned at the oafish, exceedingly white-skinned man who stood there, dressed up to look like a certain Labour MP Gabriella had snared into her bed several times. She had catered to the MP's sadistic fantasies, so very close to the edge.

"You're on," Derek said to the man.

The man exhaled. He was excited. It was the look of a man about to go into a battle, a man wrestling with some very personal demons.

"Come on," Derek said, ushering him out into the hallway. "Break a leg."

The other man laughed. It was a fake laugh, but Derek enjoyed it just the same. That was one of the benefits of being in a position with leverage, head of an empire, or something even more powerful, something the world was going to quake at, Shock Troupe. The luxury was that people always did what you wanted them to.

They walked together down to the bedroom door and knocked once.

Gabriella was slow to rise from the bed, but finally Martin could hear her approach the door. She opened the door, a vision in her negligee, her soft sleep-laden eyes looking up at Derek and the man with him.

Her eyes queried first Derek, then stared at the other man. She stepped back, intuitively retreating from the man with the unhealthy white pall about him. He was like something from a horror movie. Something grown in a lab that had spent its entire life indoors.

"What is it?" she said.

"This is Russ," Derek said.

Russ took out a scarf, waved it once in front of her face. Snake charmer to cobra. Gabriella backed away, recognizing the scarf. That same scarf had been wound around her neck during an S&M night with the MP.

Then Russ took out a thin, jeweled dagger and proudly showed her the point.

"What's going on?" she said.

"Russ is going to make you a star," Derek said. "In your biggest—" he lowered his head sadly "—but, unfortunately, your *final* role."

3

The phone call from London to Amsterdam cost Walker Jessup a quarter of a million dollars. That was the contract price of the man who arrived at London City Airport at nine o'clock in the evening.

Nile Barrabas had taken a short one-hour flight from Amsterdam that catered to businessmen. While the businessmen pored over spread-sheet hieroglyphics to divine their company futures, Nile Barrabas fended off the devotions of a flight attendant named Karen, a tawny-haired girl with a pixieish face and a devilish figure.

She'd managed to convey in a short amount of time which hotel she was staying at and her keen interest in a certain type of man—like the one in the leather jacket, the man with a weathered face and a shock of white hair, a man most certainly damned but sitting there with a don't-give-a-damn air just the same.

Barrabas looked nothing like a businessman, even though he did run a very specialized business. It was a business where the end product often was sudden death.

His business associates were known—to the very few in the know—as the Soldiers of Barrabas. They were veteran hell-raisers all, every last man and woman.

And though Barrabas was the chief executive, each SOB took an equal hand in executing the contract.

Colonel Barrabas, an irregular officer of an elite band of mercenaries, was still very much in command. And *The War* was still on. It was an endless war fought on constantly shifting fronts where the enemy rarely wore uniforms.

The SOBs were for hire, but only for red-white-and-blue work. Unlike some mercs who were for sale to anyone, the SOBs looked after American interests, highly paid players in the Patriot Game.

The stewardess hovered near Barrabas again, dropping her hand gently on his shoulder just as he was about to get up from his seat. "And where did you say you were staying?" she asked.

"Actually," Barrabas said, "I didn't."

"Oh."

"I like to stay with friends whenever I'm in town," he said.

Her moist red lips parted in a half smile, revealing gleaming teeth. "Well," she said, grasping his hand with more of a caress than a handshake. "Let's hope we become friends."

Barrabas smiled, then moved down the aisle. Another time he might have pursued her, but he'd just spent two weeks in Amsterdam with Erika Dykstra, a sparkling blond gem who stood out even in Amsterdam's diamond district.

When the call had come from Walker Jessup, a former CIA operative known as the Fixer, who now ran his own covert missions, Barrabas was idling in the hotel suite overlooking the Amstel River that he and Erika shared during his stays. She was due back soon from a business dinner related to her thriving import-export business.

But Jessup was about to launch an operation.

So despite the incandescent beauty of Erika, it took no time at all for Barrabas to say yes to the operation. When Jessup called it was never social. It meant battle lines were being drawn.

Barrabas left Erika a goodbye note under the straw-handled pewter tea service he'd bought her in a shop on Muntplein. The note was a hastily inked gesture of love that said duty called. They had had their shares of troubles, but that was the way it was with them. They didn't have much of a future, but they had one hell of a present when they were together.

Even without the mission, Barrabas would have left her soon. Paradise was boring. Like a modern-day Adam, he would have plucked the fruit just to get the hell out of the garden.

Barrabas exited the plane, Eden behind him, hell before him, and twenty minutes later he was in a taxi heading toward the heart of London.

When they reached the Camden Town district, Nile grabbed his leather travel bag and said, "Let me out here."

"But it's a Mayfair address you gave me," the driver said. "Innit?"

"It is," Nile agreed. "But I've got some idling time." And perhaps, he thought, after his meeting with Jessup, he'd have to rev up the engines.

The balding, fiftyish driver pulled over to the side of the road, shaking his head at the young and not-so-young street crawlers spilling in and out of the rock clubs. "There's a lotta nutters about. It's not the safest place here."

Nile laughed, listening to the boisterous shrieks and shouts of the fuel-injected crowd milling about. He'd been in worse combat zones than that. "I'll survive," he said.

He paid the driver and stepped out. He had to stretch his legs. The flight from Amsterdam, the taxi ride and the impending sit-down with Walker Jessup involved too much inactivity for his tastes. He'd been living in slow motion for too long recently and had to move around.

Camden Town, a downscale haven for rockers of all creeds and colors, was a good place to start.

Nile passed a group of Goths holding up the brick facade of a nightclub with painted black windows. Both the guys *and* girls wore stiletto boots and brightly colored fright wigs. The girls, their faces streaked with war paint, had poured themselves into quick-molding jeans or wore short parachute skirts. Their fancy plumage made them look like exotic birds who'd escaped their cages and were fluttering around aimlessly in the streets.

Some were striking, some looked struck.

Nile was never surprised by the styles sported by London's disaffected youth. With so many of them out of work, they had plenty of time to dress up for the endless street masquerade, always on the lookout for the next fashion cult to join, the next song about anarchy to dance to.

Nile walked slowly through the mews and backstreets, stopping off at a Salisbury pub in the theater district. He propped up the bar just long enough to drink a half pint of lager before setting out for his rendezvous with Walker Jessup.

At two minutes to eleven he rang the bell of a Georgian town house at Bryanston Square in Mayfair, an area populated by a quiet elite of former and current intelligence operatives.

Sprinkled throughout Mayfair were a considerable number of embassies, luxury homes, expensive shops and a few elegantly hidden military headquarters for both British and American outfits.

It was a natural habitat for a man like Walker Jessup, who had residences, offices and contacts in just about every arena of the international spy and mercenary network. Jessup had gone from CIA to CEO, running a covert industry that left invisible footprints from Washington, D.C., to the far ends of the earth.

Jessup did the office work.

Nile Barrabas and his SOBs did the fieldwork.

A man Nile hadn't seen before opened the door to the town house. But it was obvious he'd been expecting somebody fitting Nile's description.

He'd also been ready for anyone else, judging from the way his blue suit was tailored for quick access to his shoulder holster. He nodded at Barrabas as if he were an old friend.

"Come in," he said. "He's waiting for you in—"

"The dining room," Nile said.

The man laughed. "I see you know Jessup well." He spoke without a trace of an accent. Either he'd forsaken his British accent, or he buried it as the occasion demanded. His short brown hair was smacked neatly in place. He looked like a very proper and, Nile guessed, dangerous man.

"Brendan Laird," the man said, introducing himself. "I'm acting as liaison."

"With whom?" Nile said.

"Whomever you need," he said. "This way."

Nile followed him down the hall, wondering if he was SAS, Special Branch, Blue Beret or M16. The man could be affiliated with any of those outfits, or all of them, he thought.

Laird stopped outside the dining room and waved his hand in the direction of the door. "I'll stay out here," he said.

Nile stepped inside and closed the door behind him.

At the end of a graceful but solid-looking dining table sat Walker Jessup. His head was bent as though he were looking for his reflection in the highly polished wood surface. The table was spread with all manner of dainties, but Jessup was cradling a solitary cup of tea. He was slimmer than he had been for years, and his features bore the marks of an inner conflict.

He looked up balefully at last and emitted a muffled hello.

Nile surveyed him in silence for a minute more, then pulled a ladder-back chair from the long dining table. "What's going on?" he asked.

"Hungry?" Jessup parried.

"No."

"Shouldn't let that stop you," Jessup said.

"Yeah, well." Nile dismissed the suggestion with a wave of his hand that it was time to get to the issue without the interference of minor things like food. Action loomed on the horizon, and it had to become the focus of attention.

Jessup used to work in the field. Back in Nam, then in an assortment of other hells flaming around the earth. He'd been a good soldier in those days, a good controller. But the steel in his spine had moved upward to his brain.

His mind was still a precise and deadly machine. But at one point his body had become an exotic ruin supported by shaky pillars of fine cuisine and finer wines. Lately he'd made some recovery in that direction, but whether he'd persevere was unsure.

But that didn't make him, nor had it ever made him, a pushover.

Barrabas clasped his fingers together and rested them on the table. "Let's get down to it," he said.

Jessup nodded. "It's the usual for starters. Two hundred and fifty grand for each SOB. You'll need 'em all. Start rounding them up from whatever saloons they're laying seige to."

"It's in the works," Barrabas said.

"Good," Jessup said. "Now it gets kind of unusual."

The fat man pushed aside his cup after a last longing look at the dishes on the table, then got up. He wheeled over a rolling tower of video decks capped by a large television monitor, tugging it behind him as though it was as light as a baby stroller.

He positioned it midway down the table so they both could see it. Then he dropped back into his chair, cradling a remote control box in his hand.

He zapped the television on, pressed the play button and fast-forwarded the videotape until a two-word title appeared on screen. The words GUERRILLA

THEATER were superimposed over a Mercedes-Benz riding through a lush green English countryside.

Barrabas shook his head. "Don't tell me you brought me here so we could play a 'Siskel and Ebert at the movies' number."

"Just watch. It's not your average movie."

Nile nodded. He didn't say another word. He didn't have to. The movie spoke for itself. It spoke loudly, starting with footage of an actual killing that had just recently shocked the capital.

The first scene showed a well-known Labour MP getting out of his car. The philandering MP, nicknamed the "Red Rooster" by the press, had been involved in sensitive defense issues in the U.K.

The second scene showed the obese MP cavorting in bed with a beautiful blond woman who administered to his kinks.

The third scene was a grisly snuff tableau showing the MP carving up the blond.

Barrabas gripped the table, his knuckles turned white with rage at the brutish slaughter. He wanted to destroy the MP.

The movie obliged him.

The fourth scene showed the MP getting whacked with a 9 mm burst from a passing car as he stepped out of his favorite restaurant. He spun around several times in a bloody waddling death.

"A well-choreographed assassination," Barrabas said. "And, from the looks of it, well deserved. Was all of it real?"

"At first glance, yes," Jessup said. "I've got some people going over the snuff scene to see if it was a stand-in or the Red Rooster." He exhaled loudly, then said, "The point is, it *looks* real. This is a professional film. Keep watching."

The "documentary" continued, showing several unsolved murders and assassinations. The targets were mostly political or military figures. Every hit was *justified* by spliced-in footage showing the targets involved in every imaginable type of ruthless criminal activity.

Subconsciously the mind came to accept that every target shown on the screen was guilty of a heinous crime, proof positive that they got what was coming to them. The theme of the film was that someone was finally dispensing justice to the corrupt wheelers and dealers in power.

"Who made this thing?" Barrabas asked. "Robin Hood?"

"That's what they want you to think," Jessup said, hitting the *Pause* button. "As propaganda, it's perfect. When you analyze the targets, you see that nearly everyone of them was connected to joint U.S.-British defense operations."

"Quite a coincidence," Barrabas remarked.

Jessup nodded in agreement and started up the tape again.

The film continued its litany of corruption, revealing corrupt faces behind the public masks of prominent British and American citizens. After a few more minutes, Jessup paused the tape on the single credit that appeared on the end of the film—A "SHOCK TROUPE" PRODUCTION.

"What do you make of it?" Jessup asked.

"Disinformation, propaganda, mixed with a lot of truth. It's a powerful package."

"There's a new videotape phenomena called 'Death Tapes,' making the rounds in video stores," Jessup said. "Actual footage of suicides, accidents and plane crashes. Real life victims of carnage are packaged into video collections and presented as entertainment."

"Circus Maximus," Barrabas said, thinking of the ancient life-and-death spectacles favored by the Romans.

"In a way," Jessup agreed. "But Shock Troupe takes it one step further. Staged killings. Live assassinations on videotape. They're tapping into the culture, trying to make folk heroes out of themselves in the process."

Barrabas was growing impatient. He agreed that what he had witnessed was an outrage, but disinformation, propaganda and bodyguarding weren't his line of work. "Walker," he said. "I think you need some spooks for this, not troops."

Jessup lifted his hand. "Spooks are all over this one. But you're wrong about troops. I need an army this time around. A small army."

"Convince me," Barrabas said.

"A picture is worth a thousand words," Jessup said, pressing the remote box. Once again the videotape played on-screen.

The screen faded to black. After a couple of seconds, *COMING ATTRACTIONS* appeared onscreen.

Like a military travelogue, the tape showed several U.S. military bases in England, dwelling on overt and covert stations in Cheltenham, Harrogate, Chicksands and Haverfordwest. It then panned a series of embassy flats and safehouses maintained by the U.S.

Faces of CIA, NSA and DIA personnel flashed on the screen one after the other. Appearing beneath the faces in red typeface was a blunt warning:

WAR CRIMINALS
DESERVE
WAR JUSTICE

Jessup stared at Barrabas with an expression that indicated he'd looked reality in the eyes and had come away shaken. It was a look of full comprehension of an awful probability. "Shock Troupe will hit these people one by one. And you can bet they'll manufacture evidence justifying their actions, ending up heroes in the bargain. It could destabilize U.S.-U.K. operations."

"All right," Barrabas said. "I've seen enough."

"Wait, there's one more," Jessup said, nodding at the videotape as he let it roll.

The familiar landmarks of Fort Meade, Maryland appeared. Then the camera zoomed in on the Puzzle Palace, the "secret city" headquarters of the NSA. Several different locations flashed on-screen, finally settling on a Baltimore suburb where an athletic-looking man in a three-piece suit hurried from his colonial home to a waiting limo.

Although at first glance his spectacles and neatly trimmed beard gave him the appearance of a college professor, a close-up of his face as he dropped into the limo had "spook" written all over it.

"Tsar Nicholas," Barrabas said, recognizing the second in command to DIRNSA, the director of the National Security Agency.

"The one and only," Jessup said.

Teddy Nicholas, nicknamed "the Tsar" because of his expertise on the Russians, was the man working behind the scenes to keep the U.S. relationship with the British on a strong footing.

Tsar Nicholas was also their main link with the covert powers in Washington. Without him around to pull the right strings, a lot of SOB operations would be dead in the water.

Barrabas was aware of the Tsar's hand in past SOB operations. Hell, it was one of the few hands in Washington that would pull the trigger on terrorists by okaying an SOB mission.

"It's pretty clear what Shock Troupe is," Jessup said. "An underground army, a well-outfitted terrorist group with a sophisticated political and military capacity. First indications point to an Active Measures operation gone independent. The KGB planted a few seeds and let it grow."

He fell quiet, grimacing as if the thought gave him indigestion. "Shock Troupe is a mutant offspring, a virulent, successful one, and unless we stop it here in the U.K., it's going to spread to the U.S."

Barrabas stood as the videotape came to an end. It was like a résumé. Shock Troupe was advertising its abilities to the world, announcing that it was ready to go to work.

Nile Barrabas carried his own résumé with him. It was written in invisible ink, scar tissue crisscrossing his body in a covert map that traced his campaigns from the day he grabbed the skid on the last chopper flying out of Vietnam.

"The U.S. has been given carte blanche on this one. Within reason. It's too politically sensitive for SAS, although we do have an in with them.'' Jessup nodded toward the door, and Barrabas knew he was referring to Brendan Laird.

U.S. agencies were always allowed to handle their own security in the U.K., if only because of the great expense involved. But Barrabas sat through the rest of the briefing, knowing that Jessup believed in overkill when it came to intelligence.

"We're getting a lot of intel on Shock Troupe locations, arms and fighters. Some of it is tainted, but some good. Apparently they have a lot of enemies as well as friends. We'll know soon enough. One thing for sure is that they've got some damn good troops working for them. When the time comes, I want the SOBs ready to hit them."

"Fine," Barrabas said, rapping his hand on the table for emphasis. He headed for the door before Jessup could snare him any longer. "I'll get my people organized."

"You understand what I want?" Jessup asked, his gaze meeting the mercenary leader's directly.

"Sure," Barrabas said, nodding his head at The Fixer. "You want the SOBs to invade England."

4

Alex Nanos emerged from the underground station at Piccadilly Circus in the middle of a crowd of urgent sightseers. The sights were of the moving kind, London streetwalkers who flitted about like brightly colored birds of pay, while promising to perform some of the most amazing acrobatics in the world.

Nanos felt right at home with the statue of Eros looming above him. At least there was someone in London he was well acquainted with.

The air was cool and heavy with impending rain as he made his way through the disciples of Eros who'd gathered around the statue, looking for someone to share their faith for a half hour or so. But Nanos had been practicing his own form of worship for several weeks now in the Florida Keys aboard the boat that was now second home to the Coast Guard vet.

The Greek-American seaman believed his body was a temple, women's bodies were altars, and it was his god-given duty to worship whenever the chance arose.

He'd been especially devout during the most recent sun-and-sin cruise.

Perhaps too devout.

Alex Nanos was always at war, whether it was the SOB operations he undertook for Nile Barrabas or the war between the sexes. Whatever the arena, Nanos was an expert in unconventional tactics.

His armory for that was the weight lifter's body which he always pushed to the limit. But unfortunately, he tilted his elbow and chased women just as hard as he trained, which accounted for the hint of pallor on his normally swarthy complexion.

Nanos dodged artfully through the crowds, which at this time of day seemed like a good portion of the Western World.

He carried with him nothing but a hangover permanently imprinted on his brain, the clothes on his back, and a small canvas travel bag.

Whatever else he needed would be provided by the shops in London or the spook service they were working for. He had no idea what the assignment was. Barrabas had just told him that Her Majesty's government needed them.

"Which majesty is that?" Nanos had said into the ship-to-shore phone the SOB chief had reached him on. A sparsely-clad brunette from Virginia had been clinging to him at the time.

"That's the $250,000 question," Barrabas said. "Figure out the answer and it's yours."

"England!" Nanos shouted.

"Sharp as ever," Barrabas said. He gave him the time and place for the rendezvous, then rang off.

The brunette had kissed Nanos goodbye at great length, and Alex Nanos went off to England to work for Her Majesty. Of course Her Majesty would not even be aware of it. Only the British service that called on the SOBs would know of their existence.

With Jessup as the contact man between the NSA and the SOBs, the mission most likely affected the U.S. more than the U.K. They wouldn't be involved unless it was in the best interests of the U.S.

Like the other SOBs, Nanos had been chosen as much for his skills as for his heart. He always came down on the right side, never taking operations that could hurt the U.S. in any way.

Alex Nanos was still part of an army, a secret army that fought secret wars.

He headed up Regent Street, familiar with the area from past sojourns in Britain. It was a good place to get his bearings.

The Greek SOB proceeded past the landmarks of Mayfair he'd previously seen from the inside looking out. The U.S. embassy in Grosvenor Square, the swank hotels for the string-pullers of the world.

The rendezvous with the SOBs wouldn't be in Mayfair. It wouldn't do to have a group of American mercenaries landing on such an elegant beachhead. One or two could get by, yes. Separately they could blend in with the background, but the whole crew would stand out more than was desirable. Too many people watched what went on in that area. Together, the SOBs could easily be noticed and remembered.

Nanos would most likely be remembered as the wall that walked. His physique had been pumped up for years, although he never went overboard. He still kept himself in fighting trim. Unlike many lifters who bulked up too much, Nanos favored fluidity more than mass. He kept himself at full strength, but it was a strength he was able to move fast with and use.

A double-decker bus careened to a stop in front of Nanos, spilling a stiff measure of Londoners onto the street. Though he could navigate anything at sea, he'd quickly tired of sailing through crowds. Since it wouldn't be proper to wade through and leave a few of them sitting on the pavement, he summoned a taxi.

A black cab pulled over and scooped up Nanos.

"Where to?"

"The Florida Keys," Nanos said, sinking into the seat.

"That'll cost you a bit extra, mate."

"Never mind then," Nanos said. He gave the address of the hotel by King's Cross Road that Barrabas had chosen for the rendezvous.

He sat back, knowing that once he got to his leader there would be little chance for that.

CLAUDE HAYES looked like an ambassador as he walked up Gray's Inn Road from Holborn.

The elegantly dressed black man had just returned from a short stopover in Paris, after a tour of Mozambique and Nigeria, some of his favored haunts from his pre-SOB days.

Things had changed. But things were always changing in Africa. That was the only thing that remained a constant.

The specialist in underwater demolition had spent a lot of time on the African continent after his stint with the U.S. Navy. He'd soldiered for FRELIMO in Mozambique as a guerrilla chieftain, and later opened up a diving school and charter fishing outfit in Lagos, Nigeria.

The fishing was slow, and so was life in general when Nile Barrabas recruited the Navy vet.

Though Claude Hayes had moved as far away from the Detroit suburbs as possible, and though he'd vanished for years in Africa, it wasn't hard for Nile Barrabas to find him. Barrabas always got what he was looking for.

He'd needed a man with Hayes's martial and mental talents for a rescue operation for Joseph Noboctu, the kidnapped African patriot. Ever since that first operation, Claude Hayes had found the movable home he'd been looking for.

With the SOBs there was always a cause, a cause that this time around brought him to London.

Claude savored the looks he received from men and women alike as they tried to place him. Was he someone they should know? Or was he someone dangerous, someone they wouldn't want to know if they were on the wrong side?

Though he usually dressed casually, today Claude Hayes was returning from an embassy affair in Paris. He hadn't cared much for the embassy, but he'd certainly enjoyed the affair with the soft-skinned daughter of an Egyptian dignitary he knew from his past.

Hence the diplomatic duds.

He hadn't really had time to change, and so the persona that flew in from Paris a short time ago was that of a man who breathed the rarified airs of the embassy.

Diplomat or banker would be the most likely guess, he thought, studying the inquisitive looks of passing women, looks that were designed to size him up. But would anybody think that he was a soldier? Perhaps some of the men who'd been in the same line of work would discern his military background.

Whoever or whatever they thought he was, there was one thing clear. Claude Hayes was a substantial man.

Though he could speak several dialects, he could also speak one of the strangest of all—the King's English. The very, very tony talk of the upper caste.

Perhaps here it would come in handy. The King's English was still very much in evidence among the British Intelligence services, although the gates had recently been opened to admit more people from all of the classes into the club.

As if he'd been walking by instinct, the hotel right near King's Cross Road appeared in front of him, smooth and sleek and modern.

The moment he passed through the plushly carpeted lobby, Claude Hayes abandoned the diplomatic demeanor. A mission was in the works and the masquerade was over.

Like Claude, the rest of the SOBs were immune to bullshit.

WILLIAM STARFOOT II, the Osage Indian otherwise known as Billy Two, also flew into London to meet the SOBs.

Despite Alex Nanos's longstanding barb that Billy Two was fleet of foot but light of head, the Osage Indian came in by plane rather than astral projection.

Ever since he'd fallen into the hands of the Russians during a deep penetration mission, Billy Two had not been quite the same. The experimental drugs he'd been subjected to worked their black and white magic on him, leaving him adrift in an ocean of madness and mysticism.

He recovered in stages, sometimes through the help of Lee Hatton, the only female and only doc on the SOBs team. But more often than not it was up to Billy Two himself to fight his way through the fog that still settled around him from time to time.

And of course, there was one more entity who helped—Hawk Spirit.

He seldom spoke of the awakening of Hawk Spirit inside of him, the mythic and mystic Atlas of his soul who helped keep him aloft during the brain-burning aftermath of the experimental drugs that sapped him.

Billy Two didn't *have* to speak of it anymore. The others accepted this aspect of Billy Two with little fear, and knew that it was with him all the time.

In fact, instead of harming the SOB operations, there were moments when Billy Two's Hawk Spirit actually helped them. Though the soldiers considered it more of an instinct or battle savvy that propelled the Osage guerrilla tactician and martial artist, if he wanted to call it Hawk Spirit no one was going to argue.

It was no great kindess to allow Billy Two to stay in the SOBs. He and Hawk Spirit added up to one hell of a soldier.

His soldiering skills had stayed with him from his Marine days. So had his physique. Billy Two's martial arts training and his treks through the Oklahoma wildlands kept him in peak condition.

He was dressed in jeans, thin-soled leather boots, and his long black hair was drawn taut along the sides and tucked into the collar of his lightweight khaki windbreaker.

London had become a melting pot of nationalities these past couple of decades, as former subjects of the far-flung Crown sought refuge in the colonizing country from their revolution-wracked lands. But even with the mix of people swarming through Hyde Park, Billy Two's distinctive American Indian ancestry stood out.

Unlike the American Indians who were brought over to London in the glory days of the empire to be paraded on exhibition as noble savages, Billy Two had come to keep the empire from fading away.

"And drink is a draught of winter in the body, eternity's chill warning..."

A small crowd had gathered at the Speaker's Corner in Hyde Park where Park Lane and Bayswater Road met. A seasoned haranguer on the evils of drink was hiccupping between rounds of applause.

Like his American kin, television evangelists who screamed about the hellfires of fornication while indulging in whatever they could on the side, the British orator had obviously sampled several stiff drinks before getting up to speak against the ills of alcohol.

It wasn't the message that counted, though. It was the messenger.

He had a strong well-clipped voice that carried over the mixed crowd of Londoners, drowning out the occasional squawking of skinheads who couldn't deal with anything more complicated than four-letter expletives.

Billy Two paused for a few minutes to listen to the orator detail all of the dangers of drink and how it could turn otherwise normal men into mindless brutes.

He probably met Nanos, Billy Two thought, pushing a couple of leather-jacketed skinheads out of his way as he headed down Oxford Street.

THE WENCH'S COSTUME was favored by barmaids the world over, but in the Bloomsbury pub, it really seemed right in place.

Especially on the barmaid serving Liam O'Toole. Her low-cut square bodice was as full of figure as O'Toole's mug was of ale.

He was holding himself to just a quick one today. The meet with Barrabas and the crew would soon begin. And O'Toole's long-reigning quest for fast-flowing drink and fallen women would have to end.

Although O'Toole had tried many of his best gambits, the barmaid was immune to the red-haired Irishman. Or maybe it was just the atmosphere. The dark wood pub had probably echoed with every line or limerick in the book for the past two hundred years.

He finished his drink, then, more to see her than have another drink, caught her eye with the raised mug.

"It's almost enough to make me give up poetry," Liam said when she returned and leaned over the table to slide another full mug in front of him.

"You're a poet?" she said.

"At times I think so," he said. "Though the rest of the world doesn't."

"Well, don't go by that," she said. She put her hand on her hip, confronting the weathered muse. "If I went by what everyone thought, I'd be popping home to bed with every man jack in here. Every sod who comes in the pub thinks that just because I work here and wear this—'' she nodded towards the revealing barmaid's bodice ''—I'm here for their amusement, for God's sakes.''

''Terrible how some blokes think,'' O'Toole said.

''Isn't it?'' she said, evaluating the specimen before her. A broad-chested redheaded sonnet-spinning Irishman. Or was he? The question lingered in her eyes.

O'Toole met her gaze with the best mask of innocence a rogue was capable of.

''Are you writing now?'' she asked.

''Always,'' he said.

She looked around the pub. It was thriving with customers. ''Well, I'm too busy now, but come back sometime when it's thinner, and we'll talk.''

''Aye,'' he said. Talk they would. And talk and talk and talk. And perhaps their conversation would evolve to the language that needed no words. The language that she professed to despise.

O'Toole left the half-finished mug on the table, along with a considerable tip, then walked out of the pub and strolled by the ornate galleries, the somber but regal buildings and the hallowed heart of London University.

He'd chosen Bloomsbury for his farewell drink to the writing life because it was the center for a good many London publishers. Not that he expected any of them to publish him, of course. O'Toole's work was decidedly out of style.

Beowulf, Idylls of the King, those epics were his métier.

Though not yet a Tennyson idylling away his time with royal patronage, O'Toole knew a few Galahads of his own who had prominent roles in his epics. And while the SOBs were not quite knights in shining armor, they were armored knights working for their own brand of chivalry. Free-lancers, O'Toole thought, in the original sense of the word. Lances for hire.

The original poets were soldiers first, bards second. Like Taliesin, like Malory, they sung the songs of their captains, the deeds that raised them in battle or led to their berths underground.

And that was out of style.

O'Toole, though, was never one to go with the crowd. True, he'd come close to having his visions put between covers. A soldier of the silver screen had commissioned some of his work to form the backbone of a war epic, but that hadn't worked out to O'Toole's satisfaction. And there was an occasionally interested small-press publisher in New York who encouraged O'Toole's work but wanted more of it before she could commit.

By the time he satisfied her, he'd be ready to be committed.

With the fees he earned from the SOBs, the former Army captain could have easily put out a chapbook or two, or ten thousand if he wanted. But he wanted it the right way; the only way. He wanted somebody to *want* his poetry.

It would have to wait, though, he thought as he headed toward the rendezvous. It was time to put away the poems and plowshares and bring out the swords.

LEE HATTON'S REFLECTION flickered across the shop windows of Soho as she high-heeled it to her mid-afternoon destination.

A steady wind pursued her, wrapping her skirt around her, enticingly molding the billowy material to her long legs.

She looked every inch the model, statuesque enough to wear the high-priced garb featured in the display windows, but too lively to ever sit still for the model's life.

Lee Hatton was a combat doctor.

She was also an SOB, fully trained in medical as well as martial arts. If the occasion demanded, she could break heads. She could also turn them.

An unwitting collector of hearts, minds and bodies around the world, her overall tan hinted at the portion of the globe she'd just come from. At Barrabas's summons she'd traded in the sun and sand of Spain for the lightening gloom of England.

Capping her Mediterranean appeal was her recently adopted Cleopatra look. Her dark hair was cut short, and there was a touch of mascara on her eyelids. Not much. Just a subtle hint of color. Enough mystery already gazed from her eyes, mysteries that could be solved only by very few men.

One of them who could was Nile Barrabas, although it wouldn't happen. Not now. Not during a mission. Barrabas didn't want her for her looks—although that could come in handy. He wanted her for her skills. She was a full-fledged member of the team,

ever since Nile had first used her services when he
teamed up with Walker Jessup.

Jessup had "volunteered" Lee Hatton's services on
that first SOB mission.

Barrabas had accepted begrudgingly; then he saw
her in action and found out that she was a born SOB.

NILE BARRABAS STOOD at the end of a long glossy
conference table. The table wasn't quite fashioned
from the mahogany or aged oak of kings. It was
forged with the Formica of businessmen.

After all it was a functional hotel. Nothing fancy.
Just suitable enough for small meetings like the current one. The room was equipped with the appropriate hardware, including a solid array of video decks
and projection screens.

What the hotel had going for it was its relative ob-
scurity.

Walker Jessup had made the arrangements through
Brendan Laird, the SAS contact man who swept it for
bugs. In the spirit of international trust shown by all
intelligence services, Jessup then brought in an NSA
tech man to sweep the room again and remove any
devices that might have been left there during Laird's
debugging.

The room was clean, bringing the services one step
closer to real trust.

It was standard procedure. The U.S. considered the
British services penetrated by the Soviets and their
satellites at all levels. And the British assumed likewise about the Americans.

It was a necessary assumption and, more times than
either side cared to admit, painfully true.

The SOBs were gathered about the table, waiting for the briefing that would inform them why they were all assembled once again.

Barrabas had given them plenty of time to say their hellos and get in their digs at one another before starting off.

"It's nice to see you all here again," Barrabas said. "Alive and well and—" he shot a look at Nanos who'd been walking around the room, clandestinely inspecting it for a hidden bar "—and sober."

Nanos smiled and said, "Always."

A chorus of laughter peeled away Nanos's pretended innocence.

"Perhaps just a few from time to time," Nanos added, standing behind his seat like tarnished royalty. "But the last drink was a few days ago. Since then I've been training every day. Two hundred push-ups a day..."

"On whom?" Lee Hatton said.

"A gentleman never tells," Nanos said, slipping into his seat.

"And you can never tell a gentleman," Lee said.

Claude Hayes sat by the end of the table near Barrabas. O'Toole and Billy Two had taken positions midway down the table on opposite sides, like two bookends of solid muscle and just a bit of madness. All three of them had already interrogated Nanos at length about his latest binge among the dangerous bikini-infested waters of Florida.

At one time or another they'd all experienced the delights and dangers of one of the Greek's cruises. The cruises, with an ever-changing crew of adventurous women, usually went on and on until the money ran out, or through some slight misunderstanding, which the authorities liked to call a riot, the entire crew would land in jail.

An off-duty tour with Nanos was like Club Med and roller derby mixed into one.

Barrabas looked over the team in turn, making eye contact with everyone. The recreation was over. The mission had begun.

"The reason we're here," Barrabas said, "is because of an outfit called Shock Troupe. They've committed a number of terrorist acts in Britain and most likely other points in Europe. In one form or another you've probably seen their work on television."

"Never heard the name before," O'Toole said. "Shock Troupe. That's something I'd remember."

Barrabas nodded. "That'll change soon. So far they haven't taken credit for most of their work. But its about to hit the media in a big way. I'll get to that in a bit. But first I want you to understand more about the methods they're using."

He paused for a moment, sensing that this was their time, the calm before the storm. Now he could rationally discuss the underground army they were about to face. Shock Troupe had established an almost clockwork pattern of terrorist actions, as if they were operating on a certain timetable.

According to that pattern they were due for another outrage anytime. He hoped by then the SOBs would be in the field. They had to knock out Shock Troupe before the movement picked up steam. If not, they would be involved in a guerrilla war in the streets of London.

"Until now the one thing that's been constant about Shock Troupe is media coverage. They always make sure their strikes are recorded by legitimate news media or else they have their own crews filming it. Whatever they do, there's always a record. This is a well-documented revolution."

Lee Hatton shrugged. "Every terrorist is a showman," she said. "Without the media they wouldn't carry out half of their hits."

"True," Barrabas said. "But no one has been *this* sophisticated. Shock Troupe plans to make a real impact when they go public. The British government has been able to keep this under wraps for a while, using the Secrecy Act to get cooperation from the media. But Shock Troupe has sent their 'documentaries' to other media outlets across Europe and the States. Once that's happened, it will be impossible to keep the British media from covering it. The British government will put their own spin on it, but the public will see it anyway."

"See what?" Nanos said. There was no trace of the recovering Lothario about him.

"This," Barrabas said, holding up a videotape. "It's a copy of a tape making the rounds of the BBC and the commercial networks, as well as the newspapers on Fleet Street and just about every major media outlet on the Continent."

Barrabas slapped the tape into the video deck set up beneath a large projection screen.

"As you'll see during the viewing, Shock Troupe makes a lot of claims for terrorist acts. Judging by what the British intel services have come up with, the claims seem legit. They aren't just a bunch of talkers.

One more thing about Shock Troupe: unlike most terrorists who run and hide when resistance comes, this troupe also plays out a military option. They've attacked bases, police stations, listening posts. And when they come up against it, they stand and fight.''

Barrabas played the tape. Right after the mocking *Guerrilla Theater* title came on, the first deaths unreeled in front of the SOBs.

They had the same reaction as Barrabas. Outwardly there was the clinical detachment as they studied the actions of their enemies. Inwardly there was a shudder at the cold-blooded atrocities Shock Troupe was capable of.

One thing was certain.

They were not involved now for pay, but were motivated on a personal level. Each SOB knew that any one of the targets in the film could just as well have been them.

Especially since one of the targets was Teddy Nicholas. Though it wasn't discussed among the SOBs, they knew that "Tsar Nicholas," as the Washington power brokers called him, was one of their chief backers. The super spook was privy to the highest level intelligence available to the U.S. through the NSA's massive "vacuum" system, which was capable of listening to just about any communications system—in the world or above it.

His position in the NSA allowed him to detect the hotspots that endangered the U.S., and his connection to Walker Jessup gave him the firefighters who could extinguish those hot spots—the SOBs.

The fact that Shock Troupe threatened to take out Teddy was, aside from the military threat, a direct challenge to the SOBs. For all practical purposes, Tsar Nicholas was their commander on this operation.

Their reps as well as their lives were on the line.

"That was their first communiqué to the public," Barrabas said, shutting off the tape of terrorist outrages and threats. "Some people are calling it a *Greatest Hits* collection. As you can see, it's designed to win the average viewer's support for the murders, sanctioning them in a way. The terrorists look like heroes. And it's in a package that the public is used to. Video. All of it perfectly choreographed, right down to the last bullet."

Billy Two shook his head, aware of the logistics they were up against. "This is a nightmare," he said. "Whoever carried out those hits has an empire behind them. It's not just a bunch of free-lancers. It's got the same punch as if a government was behind it."

"Right," Barrabas said. "They do have a lot of backing. A lot of hard intelligence fell into their hands."

"Is it a ComBloc operation?" Lee asked.

"Not completely. Or maybe I should say, not an official one. It appears that the Soviets aren't in agreement on this operation. It looks like one arm of the KGB might have helped set Shock Troupe up in England, and now another arm is trying to dismantle them."

"In other words, Ivan's robbing Pietrovich to pay Pavlov," Nanos said.

"In your words maybe," Barrabas said. "But yes. The Brits have been handed some heads on a platter. Apparently an action arm of Shock Troupe has been conveniently exposed by the Soviets. A couple of military attachés discussed the action arm in an area they knew was bugged by the internal security boys at MI5. It's a gift pure and simple. But before we or anyone act on that information, the Brits are going to check it out.''

"So some of the Russians don't like the guerrillas they've created, and they're undermining the operation," O'Toole said. He leaned forward, clasping his thick fingers together and sliding them cross the table. "Sounds like they got some of the same fuck-ups calling the shots here as we do in Washington.''

"Looks like," Barrabas agreed. "Or it could be a disinformation campaign. *Glasnost* or not, the Soviets don't go around handing over their agents for nothing. There's always a price tag. We just don't know what it is yet.''

Barrabas clued in the SOBs on the latest details that Walker Jessup had briefed him on during their most recent meeting at the Fixer's haven in Mayfair.

Although the SAS wasn't officially involved, it had a number of "standby" officers like Brendan Laird looking into the case.

They'd gone back over a list of accidents involving British and American servicemen over the past two years, along with a number of cases of muggings and robberies. Though soldiers of all stripes were known to get into more than their fair share of scrapes, the number of incidents involving personnel stationed at sensitive or strategic positions had skyrocketed.

In retrospect a good number of the suspicious incidents could be traced to Shock Troupe.

The terrorists had only shown half of the story in their tape. The incidents of outright terrorism and robbery had been left out of the video. Weapons thefts. Extortion. Entrapment. Armed robbery. Hit-and-run killings. All the standard tricks of the trade had been judiciously censored from the documentary of Shock Troupe actions.

When the British investigation began to heat up, they found several links to the Soviet presence in London. And just as they were about to threaten a mass expulsion of Soviet agents—like the purge that destroyed the KGB network in Britain in the 70s—they suddenly received a lot of unasked for intel from their Soviet counterparts.

Not only did it provide information on Shock Troupe, it told them a lot about the internal struggles between the KGB and GRU factions in Britain. When it came to bureaucratic infighting, the Soviets outclassed anyone in the West.

There would be winners and losers in this latest struggle in the Soviet network, and perhaps some of the losers would look for revenge by working for the West.

"Looks like we're stepping right into the middle of another free-for-all among the spook brigades," O'Toole said. "They're so good at covering their asses, we'll all have scorched backsides when this is over."

Barrabas didn't argue. O'Toole's assessment was right on the money. The SOBs had tangled with enough covert outfits to know that on any given day in the spook world the sky was green and the sun only came out at night. Sometimes it seemed that they'd been targeted by "friendly" services as often as the enemy ones.

But lately, with the Tsar's covert backing, they'd been able to keep their heads above the muddied and bloodied waters of espionage.

"I understand your concern," Barrabas said finally. "We're here strictly as a military operation this time. For the most part Jessup is handling the spook angle with the Brits. Our job is to go in and take out Shock Troupe once we're pointed in the right direction."

The SOBs nodded their agreement.

Taking on urban fighters was dangerous enough, but just as dangerous was the pen-and-paper brigade working behind the scenes. The gray-haired eminences of the intelligence community excelled at pulling the rug out from under you at any time, especially when there was a pit of sharpened stakes below.

Barrabas knew he would liaison with a number of intelligence types this time around—to cover the tracks of the SOBs or pick up more leads to Shock Troupe. Fortunately Barrabas knew the terrain. Several times during his medal-strewn rise to colonel, Barrabas had been assigned to intelligence and military attaché positions.

Barrabas was a past master of the intelligence game. The relentless fencing between the English services and the KGB and the Soviet satellite intelligence agencies was as regular as rain in Britain.

It was a dangerous game of give-and-take, rumor exchanges, spy swaps, polite threats and counterthreats, and now and then what appeared to be genuine friendship.

In cases like this, the Soviets fed information to the Brits through third parties. The Brits would follow the links back to the Soviets and then go about clandestinely verifying the information. If the information proved useful, then the Brits would owe the Soviets a favor or two, a favor always collected.

Despite the facade of occasional cooperation between the enemy services, there still were killings now and then. The fighting wasn't done between the agencies themselves. That was bad form. But their proxies carried out covert warfare—sometimes through terrorist groups or free-lancers, and sometimes through special forces.

With so many joint British-American operations endangered by Shock Troupe actions, there were bound to be intelligence types circling around the periphery of the SOBs, keeping tabs or taking heads.

He would handle that side of the mission as well as the combat operation, and the rest of the SOBs could concentrate on what they did best—getting the job done.

"What about Laird, the *sass* guy?" O'Toole asked, using the nickname the SAS men used among themselves. "Can we trust him as our liaison?"

"Jessup does," Barrabas said. He noted the smirks on their faces. If Jessup trusted a man it meant he was either beyond reproach, or else he was a gourmet cook.

"Yeah, but can *we* trust Laird?" O'Toole insisted.

Barrabas nodded. "I trust him," he said. He'd had the chance to take the measure of the SAS man during their brief meeting. It was second nature to Barrabas, something that occurred below the conscious level whenever he met anybody, an instinctual gaze that looked behind the eyes. From what Barrabas could tell, the only thing false about Laird was his name. Other than that he was on their side.

"We trust him," Barrabas said. "Unless he shows us otherwise. He's one of their best, and he's committed to us. But the usual deniability is still in force." Barrabas studied the faces around the room. "If things go wrong, no one knows us. No official help."

Claude shrugged. "No one knows you when you're down and out. Or dead."

"To make sure that doesn't happen to any of us, from here on in we're going to split up. I've made arrangements for us to be positioned around London."

"We've got them surrounded," Billy Two said.

Barrabas laughed. "In a way," he said. "But it also protects us. If anyone comes after us, we all won't be taken out at the same time."

Barrabas split them up into teams—Nanos and Billy Two, O'Toole and Hayes, Barrabas and Lee Hatton—and gave them the names of the respective hotels and safehouses they'd be staying at.

"From here on in we're on the clock," Barrabas said. "Everybody stays put and ready to go on a moment's notice. If something comes up and I'm not available, coordinate your movements with Lee."

"I've been trying to do that for years," Nanos said with his ritual leer.

Lee Hatton carried out her part by totally ignoring him.

Barrabas clapped his hands together, wrapping up the briefing. "That's it for now, then," he said. "Good luck and good hunting. Until we get the green light we lie low. Keep out of sight and keep safe. You'll find body armor and small arms waiting for you at your rooms. Welcome to England.''

5

The newspaper headlines played it safe at first, holding back their applause and reciting the facts as objectively as the English press could: *SHOCK TROUPE TAKES DRAMATIC STAND!*

But they didn't condemn the group. Rather there was a fascination with the videotapes making the rounds of the media. It was something new. Not just the old image of rabid terrorists gunning down helpless victims. This time a group of "patriots" had declared war on criminals. Or so the videotape showed.

GUERRILLA THEATER HITS HOME!
TERRORISTS, TYRANTS, OR HEROES?
SHOCK TROUPE JUSTICE.

The headlines showed a subtle leaning toward the message of Shock Troupe. Although the papers didn't quite endorse the guerrilla actions, they almost wished it were true. Someone or something had taken it upon itself to reach out and destroy thieves, murderers and traitors who had gotten away with their crimes until Shock Troupe went after them.

Round One went to the guerrillas. They had saturated the media. They woke up the talking heads on television who hadn't had a crisis to waffle over for quite some time now. Shock Troupe was everywhere, on-screen and in print. An instant hit.

After the tapes hit the European continent, the British press found itself in a race to expose, explain, and to sell newspapers. The broadcast media took a different tack. They had the tapes. They had the voices. In many ways they let the tapes speak for themselves.

INS, the Independent News Service, came out ahead of the pack, beating the BBC and other independent services with their total coverage.

Thomas Crowell, the figurehead who had made the INS well-known around the world, spoke with solemn dignity about the reawakened call for justice—though he was careful to add "from the right quarters." There had been abuses in the past, he claimed, mentioning the recent police scandal in Ireland and a dozen other similar cases addressed by Shock Troupe.

Thomas Crowell's face became almost as common on the television screens as excerpts from the Shock Troupe tape itself.

"It is indeed a tragedy that it has come to this," Crowell said, looking out at the camera after he presented Shock Troupe excerpts. "But the question remains: What has brought about the tragedy? The militarization and corruption of England from abroad, or the guerrilla fighters who call themselves Shock Troupe? Such questions must be answered. But first, it is time for all of us to ask such questions."

The Crowell Crusade set the stage for further debate and dissection of the Shock Troupe tapes. Soon more and more commentators found themselves leaping off the fence they had so artfully straddled in the beginning. Some were for, some were against Shock Troupe.

All in all Shock Troupe had a very respectable birthday. They were seen as heroes, soldiers, fighters for freedom.

Until now the overall British support for the Falklands War had tilted the country in a pro-military stance. The British had shown the "Argies," as they called their opponents in the war. As the years passed, the extent of covert help from the U.S. was revealed to be much greater than previously reported. That cemented the longstanding British-American relationship even more.

The result was that for a while the protests about the American presence fell off.

But now with all the publicity from the Shock Troupe tape, their presence was pointed out once again, along with the dangers they represented.

The Special Operations Forces of the U.S. Air Force and Navy came in for a lot of questioning. Their presence could only invite Shock Troupe attacks and disturb the peace in England. The Air Rescue & Recovery Squadron at Woodbridge and the Naval Special Warfare Unit at Machihanish were widely publicized.

Newspapers began carrying columns about England becoming nothing more than a U.S. base. The Logistics Support Center Europe at Kemble took a lot of flak from critics, and the recently hardened USAF sites at Lakenheath and Upper Heyford, designed to withstand nuclear-biological-chemical warfare, also suffered their share of abuse. Marine barracks and other air bases also came under close scrutiny.

Shock Troupe, despite their series of murderous attacks on British soil, had scored a huge victory in their first outing, providing endless bits of film and soundbites for the broadcast media.

Rather than arouse sympathy for the real victims of the bloody attacks, the guerrillas had cast them in the role of villains.

The war of the airwaves had commenced, and Shock Troupe were the conquering heroes.

"WATCH OUT!" Derek Martin said to his assistant director. "Here comes *The Starlet from the Black Lagoon*."

Both Martin and his vulture-thin A.D., Paul Thornton, stood bemused, even though they had enough experience with displays of the kind they were witnessing. The fire was there in Deborah Quarry's eyes for all to see, as the scarlet-haired actress skipped down the steps of her trailer and stalked barefoot across the damp cold sand.

Even when propelled by anger she was an entrancing sight. She had the face and figure of a Vegas showgirl and the heart of a mercenary—qualities that greatly endeared her to Derek Martin.

"The tempest draws nigh," he said.

Thornton shrugged. The Starlet from the Black Lagoon, as Derek had been calling her in private these past few days, had become more demanding now that the film was nearing completion.

It was only natural that she try to get the upper hand. The crew was already reshooting some crucial scenes so Martin could patch up those sections of the movie that didn't make too much sense. Of course the new scenes weren't all that crucial, since the fans of Martin's sex and sadism films weren't too demanding when it came to logic. But since the starlet was in the majority of those scenes, she overrated her importance.

Thornton remained emotionless as the actress approached, knowing that Martin considered no one indispensable in either his films, or more importantly, the covert part of his life.

A trio of seagulls darted in from the water, dive-bombing some of the debris from the crew's lunch that had blown across the sand near Deborah's feet. The sleek scavengers picked clean some of the burger wrappers, fought among themselves, then whirled back toward the sea.

Deborah had marched across the cold beach oblivious to everything and planted herself in front of Derek Martin, standing defiantly in the nipple-freezing wind like a statue, *The Unknown Actress*, confronting her tyrant of a director.

They'd had some warm weather for the shoot, but lately, a cold front had swept in from the coast, making it extremely uncomfortable for perhaps the only genuine actress in his stable.

Showers had pelted the beach all day, followed by hot sun for mercifully brief periods of time. Some of the beach bunnies were getting soaked without even going into the water.

"Hello there," Derek said.

"You and I are going to have a talk," she said, folding her arms over her chartreuse bikini, shielding her skin from more goose bumps. Then she gave a furious toss of her head toward the frigid waters of the North Sea.

"Talk," Derek said.

The Shakespearean-trained actress leveled a withering gaze at Martin and said, "You're fucking crazy if you think I'm going in the water today."

"Let's get one thing straight," Martin bellowed. His uncharacteristic show of temper snapped the heads of the film crew in his direction, and dropped an uneasy umbrella of silence around them.

The actress froze.

"I'm a *crazy* fucker," Martin said. "Not a *fucking* crazy!"

The crew broke up. They'd been expecting fireworks, only to have the director defuse the situation.

The actress stared up at him and laughed. She'd been priming herself up for this argument, planning for the showdown for a long time. The tension that was always present on any movie set had been building up steam and had to blow. The long hours of low-budget productions like this one turned even the most unassuming and grateful starlets, the species stalked so well by Derek Martin, into prima donnas.

Temporarily.

Derek Martin was the director. He'd made countless films and countless fortunes doing things as he saw fit. He didn't make that money by letting people get their way. The actresses who worked for him followed orders or they were finished in the exploitation business—not exactly a dire threat to some, but since most of them saw the exploitation flicks as necessary stepping-stones to more mainstream films, they came around to his way of thinking.

Deborah Quarry came around. Sort of. Though she still had problems with the weather, the anger was gone from her face. It was replaced by reason, and by an actress's strongest weapon, a beautiful pout.

"Look at you, for God's sakes," she said, gesturing at the windbreaker that sealed Martin off from the chill. "And *them*." She nodded at the others, all dressed in suitable clothing to keep them warm. The crew had been with Martin long enough to know that he kept a shoot going no matter how brutal the weather. He thought the elements added a realistic flavor to his films.

It was obvious that with her red hair flapping steadily in the wind that shrieked across the shoreline, and her exposed flesh shuddering with each icy breath, Deborah Quarry didn't share the director's hunger for realism.

Martin scanned the well-dressed shooting crew, approving of what he saw.

"Now look at me," she said, gesturing at the skimpy bikini selected for her.

"I'm hoping millions of fans will do just that," he said.

"I'm talking about the weather," Deborah said. "I don't want to go in there today." She pointed a slim index finger at the water, and a perceptible shiver ran along her body as if it really did contain the sea monster that, according to the script, was going to try to devour her. By the laws of survival and the laws of exploitation movies, the monster would only succeed in tearing off the top of her bikini with its claw.

Martin's latest flick was an "homage" to films like *The Creature from the Black Lagoon* and *Huma-*

noids from the Deep. By calling it an "homage" he could tread water in the same territory without being accused of plagiarizing anybody's material.

According to the rules of the genre, the starlet had to be menaced by some primordial monster from the depths of the ocean who wanted to destroy civilization after scaring a few starlets out of their pants.

And now his starlet didn't want to be scared.

"Why the sudden change of heart?" Martin asked. "If I recall, you were delighted at the opportunity, and I quote, 'to work with one of the greats in the field.' I believe that's how you put it."

"That was before I knew you," she said.

Martin nodded his head. His smile had changed only slightly, but the assistant director could see that his attitude toward the actress had changed. Now she really was treading in dangerous waters.

With the lewd voice of a horror movie narrator, Martin said. "Had she but known there was a slimy green tentacled monster that wanted to tear off her clothes, she might not have gone into the water. Then again, she never was too bright."

Deborah stood there, and cast an appealing glance at the assistant director in search of support, but he looked through her.

"Into the water, Deborah," Martin said.

She was about to protest, but she saw an expression come into his eyes, and she realized there were sharks on land as well as in water. There were a lot of stories about Derek Martin, stories that she had discounted until now.

But there was her self-esteem to save. After all, she had stormed out here, hell-bent on having her way.

"It doesn't feel right," she protested.

"Look," Derek said. "You're an actress. You're always saying you want to do some real acting. Well, this is your chance. Pretend its warm and you're swimming in the middle of summer. It's not spring out there. It's hot . . ."

Deborah nodded her head and looked doubtfully at the shore. "I don't know," she said.

"I do," Martin said. "You either go in the water or you'll be written out of the script. Die a gruesome death off-camera. I'll write in a long-lost sister to take your place for this scene. Besides," he said, adding some honey, "there's a lot more for you if you do this. There's another part I want to discuss with you. A real one. Do right by me, and I'll do the same for you."

In her twenty-five years, Deborah had received more than her share of promises, most of them broken. She didn't totally believe him, but if Derek Martin chose to deliver on his promise, he could boost her career. Maybe even get her on the next tier—where she'd run around in revealing heavy metal breastplates for a sword-and-sorceress movie. Or maybe even get to be a slave girl in a post-apocalyptic biker-on-the-road movie.

"I'll take you up on your kind offer," Deborah said. She stepped gamely in the direction of the shore, stopping at the spot the assistant director had blocked out for the beginning of the scene.

Derek Martin called for the man in the monster suit who'd been waiting patiently for his cue.

Adam Whitehouse was six feet tall, stocky, and had two horns on his head. He was covered from head to foot with scaly green skin that shone brightly in reptilian glory.

In the script his origin was another world that was apparently ruled over by a hierarchy of fishlike creatures who fled their planet for the waters of earth. His real origin was Liverpool. After serving his time in the army, Whitehouse fled the dying industrial town. He worked first as a carpenter for set designers, moving from one theater group to another before finally connecting with Derek Martin.

Martin's group had a reputation for using film crews in front of as well as behind the cameras. One thing led to another, with Whitehouse winning a progression of more substantial roles, until now he was ready to rise from the sea in search of scantily-clad redheads.

He was called upon to perform some bizarre tasks for Martin. But his philosophy was neatly summed up in the theory that some people led even stranger lives for less pay. For the money he was paid, Whitehouse was willing to follow orders.

His real talent lay in performing the stunts for Martin off-camera. The daylight acting was secondary. He placed no importance on it, and as a result achieved a certain naturalness that came off well in the exploitation films.

"All right, mate," Martin said to the beloved monster. "It's into the water for you."

Whitehouse nodded and hurried his webbed feet down the sand into the water. He had to be in the water longer, but he was still better off than the girl. Beneath the green body suit, he had a regular diver's suit that kept him warm long enough to ply his trade as a monster in search of buxom starlets.

"And now, Deborah, if you're ready?"

"I am."

"Good," Derek said. "Break a leg." Or a neck, he thought in secret glee. He turned to his A.D., whom he was training in handling the run-of-the-mill shoots. That would free him for the more important movies that had to be made.

"This one's yours, Paul," Derek said.

Paul Thornton nodded. "Ready to roll cameras," he said. Both cameramen were in position. One focused on the monster. The other on the girl. Later, in the cutting room, Derek would assemble the film, showing the best features of the the woman, and the worst of the monster.

"Roll 'em," Paul said.

FOUR HOURS LATER when the sun began to fade and a chain of dark clouds moved in, Derek Martin had enough film to make some kind of sense out of his horny-monster-from-the-ocean-depths flick.

At the height of the filming, several bodies had littered the beach.

The heroine, by divine right of her exceptional breasts and bright eyes, always lasted to the last frame. Deborah and her amazing breasts would survive to fight evil green monsters another day. A lot of minor actresses had bought it on the beach, however, and somewhere out there was a group of scaly monsters on their way to ravage London.

Martin didn't like to shoot on location, but since he was there he decided to make the best of it, shooting some atmospheric shots that would probably make it into one of his other films.

Normally he shot on the studio sets at his estate, but try as he might, he just wasn't clever enough or wealthy enough to build his own private ocean.

Hence the film crew had to shoot on location from time to time.

At the end of the day he felt he'd made several noble additions to the reptilian-slasher subgenre. His film would compare favorably—at least in the eyes of his fans—to *The Creature from the Black Lagoon* and *Humanoids from the Deep*.

Martin's concept was that the recent toxic spills from cargo containers in the North Sea had caused a race of sea creatures to flee from their underwater haunts and look to the dry land.

Though he directed it with his usual skill, Derek Martin wasn't totally involved. His mind was on another track, on an entirely different kind of scene he was going to direct.

After a brief pep talk and a round of drinks, Martin dismissed the cast and crew, promising them that if the weather held up, he'd try to make the following day their last day of shooting.

Deborah Quarry lingered behind for a few moments to catch some extra praise from Martin.

"Beautiful," Martin said. "You were just beautiful today."

"Thanks—I appreciate the way you showed me the right motivation today."

Derek Martin did his best not to laugh. He couldn't quite tell the starlet that her Shakespearean days were gone for good, no more the delightful roles in *Romeo and Juliet* or *Hamlet*.

Although her primary motivation in the scene had been to keep away from the rapacious claws of the horny green monster, she had given it a personal dimension with some very good screams.

"No," he said. "I should thank you. It was a nice piece of acting."

The Starlet from the Black Lagoon stood up on the tips of her toes and pecked him on the cheek, not accidentally brushing her damp bikini top against him in an attempt to send a chill up *his* spine for a change. She was bestowing her largess upon him as if she were already the star she hoped to be.

There was a chance she would move on to bigger things, he thought. But not in the movies. He had plans for her, plans that might prod her into becoming a much more effective actress offscreen. Not that she could ever match some of the bloodthirsty actresses he already had working for him. But she could play a vital role in the troupe.

Deborah Quarry skipped off toward her trailer. A few minutes later the engine of her sporty red convertible coughed and sputtered, and she swung out onto one of the main roads back to civilization.

The technicians had already wrapped up their gear, and they too were headed back to town. Except for the watchman Martin had assigned to look after the trailer and other gear, Martin was left alone with his real crew.

Whitehouse approached him. Without the green body suit, he looked almost like a leading man. Almost. He had taken a few too many knocks about the head to ever pass as the clean-cut hero. Still, Whitehouse had the rough good looks that some women fell for. Unfortunately for them, Martin thought, some of them never got up again, which made Adam White-house a useful man to have around.

Paul Thornton joined them. "Well?" the A.D. said. "Shall we go block out our next scene one more time?"

"Yes," Martin agreed. "One more time." His voice was tired, but they couldn't afford to make any mistakes tonight. There was only one take. It either came off perfectly in the first reel, played without a hitch—or their act would be closed for good.

Martin was tired and wet.

The sea spray had dampened his energy all day. So had dealing with the endless needs of the cast. The showers had soaked through everyone, yet most of them had a chance to escape it at the end of the day and nurse their complaints for the rest of the night in comfort.

Martin entertained ideas of warmth, of cosy fires, down-filled duvets and toasty warm flesh heating up his. And although sleeping the night away was the utmost thing in his mind, arrangements had been made.

He'd been putting in hellish hours on the film, but then again, he had no choice. It was part of his cover. He couldn't ever cut out that part of his life. Besides, the films were a good source of income that let him do what really counted.

Tonight he had planned a double feature. He would have to grab an hour or two of sleep somewhere. It made no sense to carry out an action as if he were one of the undead who peopled his horror films. But he couldn't unwind. Not yet. According to his own sense of justice he didn't deserve it. Peace had yet to be earned.

At times like this he thought it would be nice if he could forget about Shock Troupe. Maybe one day just turn if off once and for all. But he was on a roll and unable to stop.

Martin pushed aside the tiredness.

"Come on," he said to Whitehouse and Thornton. "The show must go on."

It was time for another Shock Troupe performance.

6

Alex Nanos followed orders religiously.

Each man on the SOBs had been picked for their unique talents, and Barrabas was a master at matching each man to the mission. Which is why Alex Nanos descended upon the thriving marketplace of Piccadilly Circus at rush hour, his eyes scanning the bodies of the streetwalkers.

Following orders.

Barrabas had sent him back to his port of entry into London.

"You do know the area?" Barrabas had asked him.

"I've reconnoitered it a few times," Nanos said.

"Loitered is more like it," O'Toole said.

Barrabas had called them together for a quick meet at a coffee shop near Brompton Road, doling out assignments. While they were waiting for input from the Brits, they might as well follow up a few leads and see what they could dig up on their own.

Nanos looked every inch the man on the prowl, from his open-chested shirt—despite the rain swirling around the Eros statue—to his lust-filled eyes. That part of his cover was never too hard to manage.

A tart with purple hair zeroed in on Nanos within a minute after he cruised past the Eros statue.

The drug mart was open for business, and shoppers of all kinds, from businessmen in pin-striped suits to fading prostitutes who were trolling through the area.

But Nanos was the one to be found, and she picked him out like a hawk landing on her prey. "Want a spit-and-polish?"

She obviously wasn't referring to a shoe shine. Her matching purple-shadowed eyes proved that by moving down Nanos's body.

Even with the shock of purple that seared her once-platinum hair like a lightning bolt, she was still attractive. Her bust was exaggerated by wire upholstery and an unnaturally slim waist. The slenderness was probably a result of her habit.

Despite the supposed hunger for his body that radiated from her eyes, Nanos saw through her veil. Her real hunger was for a hit of junk to take her blues away.

"Thanks, doll," Nanos said. "But I'm looking for someone special."

"It doesn't get any more special than this, Yank," she cooed at him. A few years before her throaty voice might have worked on him. But she was too desperate now, her best years gone in a blur of dreamy memories.

"I'm sure it's a mindblowing experience," Nanos said. "But like I say, I'm in the market for someone else."

Her bedroom eyes quickly changed to suicide eyes. Nanos was just another lost bet to her, worth nothing more than a curse or two while she baited the hook again.

"You're a right gay blade, you are," she said before melting away in the crowd.

Nanos patrolled the area, ostensibly looking for another woman more to his fancy, but in reality he was looking for a script dealer who allegedly spent a lot of time near the monument.

The dealer had been picked up in a routine narcotics sweep of the Circus. The sweep wasn't designed so much to take the junkies off the street as it was to net the doctors who made their fortunes overprescribing heroin substitutes to the small army of addicts plaguing Britain.

Some of the more cynical police called the area around Piccadilly Circus "The Golden Triangle." But instead of crops, the harvest was in capsules and ampoules.

Jackie Syms was one of the junkies who'd turned in one of the docs. A relative man of honor, Jackie kept silent about the other docs who prescribed him with enough for himself and plenty left over to sell on the street. His extra junk didn't cost him a thing. That's how he stayed alive, making enough to keep his head an inch or two above the gutter.

But the London police who sweated Jackie decided he didn't have anything worth bargaining with. They already had the goods on the doc that Jackie turned in.

That's when Jackie—like junkies everywhere—offered up every last bit of information he had in order to get back onto the street. The Metropolitan Police listened with sheer boredom until Jackie told them he knew "the broad that croaked."

The "broad that croaked" turned out to be Gabriella Fucshin, the actress who was murdered in the videotape that Shock Troupe released to the media. The police took down his details on her life, although many of the officers thought it was just total fantasy. Who could trust the ravings of a drug-haunted mind?

Jackie's testimony didn't mean much at the time, since dozens of informers and petty crooks claimed to know the inside story on Gabriella. But when MI5, the Secret Intelligence Service, threw their weight into the case, they discovered that Jackie Syms really had been a part of Gabriella's life at one time.

Before Gabriella headed off for the big time and vanished into the movie world, she and Jackie were an item. That was back in the days when Jackie was an artist who just *smoked* a little heroin, chasing the dragon to get a creative edge while he painted, and Gabriella was an aspiring actress and an occasional trickster. The tricks she turned let them buy more heroin so they could chase the dragon together.

She finally kicked the habit, but the dragon kicked Jackie Syms. And Jackie kicked his painting habit when he became a full-time junkie. His life wasn't worth much anymore, but he did know some of the early details of Gabriella's entry into the actress scene. For that reason Jackie Syms was suddenly a valued informant.

The information went through the subterranean circuits of police and intelligence liaisons before finally tumbling into the hands of Brendan Laird, the SAS man coordinating details with the SOBs. Then Laird turned over the lead to Barrabas. Since Barrabas had suffered through Nanos's raptures on the denizens of Piccadilly Circus, he sent the Greek off on the mission.

Nanos lost himself in the sway of the crowd, drifting in and out of the shops, lingering in the cafés, walking up and down Shaftesbury Avenue.

Though Jackie Syms was a regular on the scene, his hours weren't all that precise. He came to deal when he was ready, sold off his extra prescriptions, then vanished.

Nanos finally zeroed in on his target shortly after the rush-hour crowds waned, picking him out from the crowd thanks to the mug shots provided to the SOBs.

Jackie Syms came up from Piccadilly Station, his hair plastered down by a combination of rain and grease. The last time it had been cut was probably one relatively straight night when he looked in a mirror and sheared off only the hair he could see. The result was a long scrambled lock of hair hanging over his jacket, like the tail of some vermin trying to find shelter in the walking shell that was Jackie Syms.

He wore a leather jacket that once held a larger man, a muscular one, in fact. But the drugs had taken care of that, and now his sole exercise was injecting himself in one of the few remaining spots on his body that would still take a hit.

His face was ravaged. He looked sallow, like something from the wax museum. But then again, he had chosen to be a wreck, living off the dole and the dope.

Nanos moved nearer to the monument, still scanning the crowd for women, talking to some of them for a couple of minutes before they passed on. He fit into the scene well enough to escape detection. Not that Jackie's senses were all that sharp in that direction.

In the space of a few minutes Jackie met with others like him, ghosts who hadn't quite taken the last train out yet. They came to deal their dipanoe hydrochloride and cyclizine hydrochloride, methadone, and dihydrocodeine. The tools of the trade.

These guys were walking pharmacies, Nanos thought. Just like Wall Streeters, they knew when the prices rose or fell by the amount of supply available. They were constantly scoring as much as they could before sinking down into their stupors again.

After Jackie looked as though he'd taken care of his business for the day, Nanos sidled over to him.

"I'd like to bargain with you."

Jackie turned and saw that the man next to him was most likely a stranger. It was hard to tell with a memory that came and went like a shorted-out radio wire. Sometimes it transmitted, sometimes there was nothing but dead air, the hiss of static. The more he looked, the more Jackie figured the newcomer as some kind of heat. Or at least some kind of trouble. He took a couple of small steps to his right.

"Don't know you, mate," he said.

Nanos closed the gap. Up close there was a scent about Jackie. It was a cloud he'd cultivated over the years. Dirt, sweat, fear. Junk. "We're old friends, Jackie," he said.

"Fuck off, Yank," Jackie said. He reached into his leather pocket.

Nanos shot his left hand out like a lever and clenched his fist around Jackie's hand. With that one hand he held the junkie anchored to the spot.

Though there were obviously some of Jackie's friends around, none of them made a move against Nanos. No one wanted to tangle with the broad shouldered guy in the gee-whiz tourist clothes.

Nanos released his grip on Jackie. "Look, I'm here as a friend." He paused, then looked down at the side pocket. "But if a knife comes out there, you'll have no more worries. Ever."

Jackie shrugged. "Promise?"

Nanos shook his head. "Come on, let's talk."

The junkie stood silent. "I said I don't know you, mate. It's dangerous to go shooting your mouth off."

Nanos gave him the name of somebody on the Metropolitan narcotics detail who had dealt with Jackie before. At the sound of the name Jackie knew that if Nanos was nosing around his turf, at least he had the approval of the man who ran him.

But he stayed silent.

"You want a beer?" Nanos asked.

The man looked blank.

"How about a cup of coffee?"

"No."

"Tea?"

A silent shake of the head greeted that offer, and ever so slightly, Jackie started to edge away from Nanos.

"Have a cup of tea with me if you want to keep walking the streets a free man."

"I already talked to every damned cop in London and his granny."

"Well I'm a long-lost cousin. Talk to me some more. It might be worth your while."

Jackie dropped his hands into his jacket pockets. He looked at Nanos, but found he couldn't wish him away.

Jackie Syms was owned by the police. It was part of the trade system. Information for freedom. If they ever needed him, they'd come looking, and if they didn't get something he would be brought in until he started sweating, and sooner or later gave them everything they wanted.

Sometimes it saved a lot of time to just get it over with on the street.

They walked a half block to a cheap-looking restaurant and dropped into a booth with a scarred tabletop. When their orders came, Jackie sipped his tea slowly. In the garish neon light, Jackie looked even more jaundiced. "What do you want?" he said.

"Gabriella Fucshin," Nanos answered.

Jackie looked at Nanos in a new light. He'd been expecting some kind of shakedown on her. "You're a bit late for that, ain't ya?"

"She's still the reason I'm here," Nanos said.

"I told everyone about her. They didn't seem all that interested at the time."

"Times change," Nanos said. "We're very interested now."

"Why?"

"I aim to get the people who did her. It was a horrible way to go."

"She was sweet," Jackie said, nodding his head, looking almost alive for the first time since Nanos saw him. There was a faint spark in his eyes, as if he were seeing their lives together again, sharing a devil-may-care bohemian paradise, both headed for stardom.

But he landed in the gutter, and she burnt out once and for all, a gruesome horror show on videotape.

"You owe her," Nanos said.

He lifted his shoulders. "Yeah, I bloody well do. But there's nothing I can do about it."

"I can," Nanos said. "Tell me who got her involved in the business. People she worked with. I'll take care of the rest."

"I'm not good at names," Jackie said. "Or places. It was a long time ago. A whole other life."

He described a few of the faces that swam up from the depths of his memory. Then his eyes suddenly reflected a bit of fire. "There was this one guy—the last guy before she left me. He came over one night, looked at me like he'd just as soon waste me. He was there to get her bags..." He summoned a few more faces before drifting off into silence.

"Do you know any assumed names she might have used?"

He thought for a minute. Then he reeled off a number of names that might or might not have been ones that she used. His memory of her starlet days was fuzzy.

"Keep the wheels spinning," Nanos said. Instead of jotting down what he heard, which would have been like hanging a neon sign on his head saying *informant*, Nanos committed everything to memory.

He led him back bit by bit to the films, asking him to describe them and the people who made them. The parties. The screenings. Even the low budget items had their ritual grand premieres. Those were the details that he pried out of Jackie Syms.

"And another movie she made for this guy," he said, "was just lots of rolling and tumbling. A bare-ass flick, but it was kind of funny. Girls with guns. Gangland girls, something like that."

The movies he described were mostly all in the same vein. A blood-spilling vein. Monster flicks full of creepy crawlies. The Brits called them "nasties." Back home in the U.S. they were called splatter, or slasher, films, the basic them being that a beautiful girl would have illicit sex just before a maniac cut her to pieces.

For a while Gabriella Fucshin led the pack in the exploitation movies, getting chopped to pieces in film after film. Until finally she got chopped to pieces for real.

After a while Jackie started shaking his head with more vigor than Nanos would have thought the man was capable of. "That's all I can tell you now," he said. "No more." He was getting agitated. Nervous. Shaky.

"Just a bit more," Nanos said.

"You want blood, don't you?"

"Yeah I do," Nanos said. "I won't bullshit you, pal. I'm talking to you so I can get to some other people. But there might be something in it for you."

"What?" he protested. "She's gone. Already gone. What can you do for me?"

"You might be next," Nanos said. "These people like to wrap up loose ends."

"Maybe they will," he said.

Nanos saw that same expression on his face again, where the threat of ending his life was of no great concern to Jackie. The world would spin around whether Jackie was on it or not.

"Maybe you don't want to live too well," Nanos said. "But you don't want to die the way she did. She didn't go out like a Hollywood heroine, pal. It took a long time for her to die."

That seemed to reach him somewhat. Even so, he wasn't motivated by fear so much as he was by need. Right then he didn't need all that much.

Nanos got him to talk a bit more, hoping that one of the details he gave about her might lead to the people behind Shock Troupe.

"What was she like, Jackie," Nanos said.

"She was beautiful," he said. "Friendly. She was for real. But she was always used. By everybody."

"Even you?" Nanos asked.

"Yeah," Jackie said. He didn't hesitate at all. He could admit anything without feeling pain. It would soon be masked by his next hit. "We're all used, man," he said. "All the time. Even now, right?"

"Right," Nanos said.

"Just so we understand each other," Jackie said. His eyes had a hollowness that affected Nanos. He was used to working the underside of the street when he had to, but it wasn't always possible to just shut out the informants and move on.

"You want out?" Nanos asked.

He laughed. "Oh, sure I do. Don't tell me you're Florence Nightingale as well as a narc. Gonna clean me up and help me go straight."

"I'm neither. But I can help if you want."

Jackie's shrug banished the suggestion into oblivion.

"One more thing before I go," Nanos said. "You got a picture of her when she was younger?"

Jackie looked guarded for the first time.

"Trust me," Nanos said.

"Why?"

"I haven't hurt you so far, have I?"

"No, but you're just getting warmed up." But even as he spoke, Jackie reached into his back pocket. He withdrew a slim and worn leather wallet, then flipped it open.

The picture jacket showed Gabriella Fucshin back when she was just starting out.

"Looks like an angel," Nanos said.

"She is an angel. For real now."

"Can I make a copy of that?"

"Sure," Jackie said. "As long as I go with you. This doesn't go anywhere I don't."

Nanos nodded. "A deal," he said. "Let's go dig up a copy machine."

Jackie handed him the photo. It was well thumbed at the edges.

"Careful," he said. "She's the only dream I got left."

Nanos nodded. If he could, he'd find the people that had turned her into a nightmare.

7

Liam O'Toole propped up the bar at the same Bloomsbury pub where he'd first met the barmaid of his dreams. Nanos was standing right beside him.

She'd noticed O'Toole immediately, and though she smiled at him, so far she hadn't had much of a chance to stop and chat. Other than finally telling him that her name was Angela, she was busy tending her customers.

The pub was filling with the crowd of regulars, some of them carried their darts with them while others carried their briefcases, then dropped them with sighs of relief on their tables.

The pub housed tourists and newcomers, as well as would-be literary greats soaking up the hallowed atmosphere.

Then there were mercenary poets like Liam O'Toole.

The boozy camaraderie drifted around him in a tempting cloud of smoke and laughter, but he wasn't able to fully enjoy it. O'Toole's presence was due to business needs. Though he'd been wanting to come back to visit Angela, he was hoping it would be strictly a social matter. Unfortunately Nanos had roused O'Toole from his hotel with an emergency call.

"Why'd you call me?" O'Toole had asked him when the Greek remained elusive on the phone.

"Barrabas has enough problems to deal with already," Nanos replied.

"That's not what I mean," O'Toole said. "What the hell can *I* do that you can't?"

"I need you to find somebody," Nanos told him.

"Who?"

"I don't know yet," Nanos said. "That's why I need you. Just meet me and I'll explain everything." He'd given O'Toole the address of a nightclub in Piccadilly Circus. The red-bearded Irishman met him a short time later. There Nanos filled him in on his talk with Jackie Syms and the early days of Gabriella Fucshin.

"So what do you need me for?" O'Toole pressed.

"I need someone who knows their way around the literary scene. A film critic or a reviewer who knows about these kind of flicks."

"Judging from the kind of movies you're talking about," O'Toole said, "you need a mortician, not a reviewer."

"This is your territory," Nanos said. "Unless you really don't know your way around the literary set..."

It was just one more dig at his poetry and his literary sensibilities. Though Nanos sympathized with his pursuit of poetry, he never stopped ribbing him about it.

And it always got the same result. O'Toole rose to the bait.

The two of them came to the Bloomsbury pub, his sole contact with the world of British belles lettres. They took a table at the back of the pub, waiting for

Angela to get a break long enough to talk. She was O'Toole's entry into the writer's milieu. The pub was a hangout for writers and critics of every stripe.

"Ahh," Nanos said. "Here she comes again. She's a beautiful one, that girl."

"Yes she is," O'Toole said. "And she's mine."

Nanos laughed. "No," he said. "You're *hers*. If she'll have you." The Greek slapped O'Toole on the shoulder and said, "I'll leave you two alone." He pushed away from the table and headed toward the dart game at the other side of the pub.

A few moments later Angela came to the table, carrying a fresh mug of lager for O'Toole and a cup of tea for herself. She pulled her chair closer to him, then dropped down beside him.

Her dark hair was swept back in an intricate braid, leaving some loose tendrils to curl around her face enticingly.

"Now then," she said. "What's this 'urgent business' you've been talking about?"

"I'd rather I came here just to see you," O'Toole said. "But there is something I've got to find out."

"Go ahead," she said.

"The last time we met—"

"The only time we met," she corrected him.

"When we met—for the only time—" O'Toole said, "you seemed to be hooked into the local literary scene."

"Ahh," she said. "So you did remember more about me than this getup." Her eyes rolled down the front of the revealing wench costume. "I didn't think you were listening to a word I said."

"I was. That's why I'm here."

"What do you want to know then?" she said. "I'm all yours."

"That's all I want to hear," O'Toole said.

"Come on, lad," she said. "Don't stop now that you've got me intrigued. What's all this talk of literary business? You going to read me one of your poems?"

O'Toole shook his head.

"What then?"

He told her about the actress. About the movies. The exploitation business.

"You mean those cheap movies with the girls showing their bums every chance they get? Is that what you're asking me about?"

"It's not for me," O'Toole said, coming as close to blushing as he'd done in a long time. "It's for a friend."

"It always is," Angela said, using the tone of voice of a woman who had heard it all.

"This time for real," he said.

She smiled. "Would that friend be the bloke who was sitting here with you?"

"Yes," O'Toole snapped. "That's it."

Angela laughed. "He did look the type to be interested in the nasties."

"He's a regular swine at times," O'Toole agreed.

She nodded. The matter was settled. O'Toole was still a tentative part of her world. "But what can I do for you?" she said. "I don't know much about those kind of movies. And I don't want to."

"That's just it," O'Toole said. "My friend needs to find an expert in those movies. A critic or a reviewer who knows all the trivia and can identify an actress who appeared in some of them.''

"Why's that?"

"She's missing." And dead to boot, he thought. But there was no need to tell her that.

"This girl needs help?"

"Yeah," O'Toole said. "She needs help." Or at least someone to avenge her.

The more he talked with Angela, the more he knew he'd chosen right. She was plugged into the literary scene more than he originally hoped for. After all, she did work in a bar that served as a prime watering hole for London's literary set.

Despite her apparent revulsion at the type of movies he'd mentioned, she knew some people who worked at the kind of magazines that covered the exploitation scene.

"I'll call around," she said, "and see if I can get something for you."

It didn't take her long. While she was gone, O'Toole examined with interest the lively bunch around him. When she returned, she slid a sheet of paper across the table with a name, address and phone number on it. She told O'Toole a bit about him then said, "This is your man," she said, the smile coming back to her face. "Or the guy who can help your friend."

"Thanks," he said. "I owe you a favor."

"That you do. And I'm sure to collect it one of these days." She gave him a slow and lazy look from beneath her eyelashes.

O'Toole's face assumed an expectant air. "Name the time," he said.

"Let me call you . . ."

He shrugged. "Can't do that."

"Oh? Afraid I'll pester you?"

"No," he said. "Not that. It's just that I have to go away for a few days. I can't be reached."

"Just what kind of poet are you?" she said. "Is all this mystery for real or are you just trying to impress me?"

"A bit of both, darling," he said. "But next time it'll be just you and me. None of this stuff." He waved the sheet of paper around.

"I'll be here," she said, slipping from her chair and heading back to work.

O'Toole followed the swirl of her skirt with longing eyes, wishing he could spend some time with her and not with *Malcolm Wainwright*, the name on the sheet she'd given him. O'Toole studied his address, then folded the paper and tucked it into his shirt pocket.

He collected Nanos from the bar, where the Greek had been occupying himself with charming yet another woman. Nanos uttered a hurried goodbye as he was pulled away. When they stepped into the outer lobby, O'Toole patted his shirt pocket and said, "Here's your man."

"Kind of small, isn't he?"

O'Toole glared at his fellow SOB. He took out the sheet of paper and tapped it against Nanos's chest. "I'm not in the mood," he said. "I may have ruined a good thing with that gal just to get this."

Nanos took the paper, unfolded it and nodded his head in approval as he looked at the name. "Good," he said. "Looks like just what we need." With a flourish he handed the paper back to O'Toole. "Call him up."

"Me? This was your idea."

"It was." Nanos agreed. "My next idea is for you to call the guy and set up a meet. Hell, you're the wordsmith, he'll listen to you. Me, he'll see through in a minute."

O'Toole shook his head. But he recognized the truth in what Nanos had said. He made the call from a telephone kiosk near the pub's entrance. After a few rings a man's voice answered. He sounded younger than O'Toole had expected, considering all of the accomplishments Angela had credited him with.

"Hello, could I speak to Malcolm Wainwright?"

"One and the same," he said.

"Good," O'Toole said. He identified himself with a cover name, then said, "I'm preparing a piece on former actresses in the exploitation field. Those who made good. Those who didn't. Where are they now and all that. I was told you're the man to see."

"I am," Wainwright said. "But I'm kind of busy right now."

Picturing Wainwright about to hang up, O'Toole said, "Of course I'll pay you for your time."

"Still, I'm transcribing an interview right now—"

"I'll pay you three times your usual rate for just an hour of your time, maybe not even that."

"Who commissioned the piece?" Wainwright asked. "Prince Charles? . . . Never mind, actually I'm more interested in who referred you to me."

O'Toole told him.

"Angela!" Wainwright spoke her name with reverence. Obviously the dark-haired Angela was a muse to more than O'Toole. "Well, in that case come right over."

O'Toole verified the address.

According to what Angela had told him, Wainwright worked as a free-lance publicist in the theater district, where he turned out a constant stream of entertainment pieces for several different magazines and newspapers. Interviews, profiles, reviews. Humor. A renaissance man of gore and movie folklore. His office was on the Strand, the street that connected Fleet Street to the entertainment district.

Leaving Nanos behind in Bloomsbury, thinking there was no sense in spooking the man who might give them a lead, O'Toole grabbed a taxi.

After a quick and mildly perilous ride, the Irishman reached the office of his quarry. It was a second-floor office with a heavy brass door knocker that looked as if it had been plundered from a haunted castle in a Hammer film.

O'Toole swung the door open and stepped into what looked like the lobby of a movie theater. To his right was a three-tiered platform that resembled a concession stand. It was covered with statues, postcards and press kits from movies O'Toole had never heard of.

"Hello?" O'Toole shouted. "This is Lee Olson!" he said, giving the phony name he'd conjured up during the earlier phone call.

"Come on in and make yourself comfortable. I'll be out in a minute." Wainwright's voice came from the end of a long hallway, floating over the sound of a computer printer kicking out some paper.

O'Toole threaded his way through the office, spying a soft plush black leather couch beside a bank of windows that looked down on the street below. The couch looked like the only item in the place not covered with movie debris. It was neutral ground.

Stacks of British film and horror magazines covered the desks and tables of his outer office. They had titles like *Fear Magazine*, *Dagon*, *Samhain*, and *Nexus*. Many of them featured scantily-clad damsels in distress. Capping one of the stacks was a hardcover book, *Scared Stiff*, by Ramsey Campbell.

Posters with lurid scenes were plastered all around the room, forming a technicolor gallery of villains and vixens. Buxom vampires and killer robots stared down at O'Toole from the wall, seeming to follow his progress as he moved through the room.

O'Toole dropped onto the couch and spread his long arms over the soft back.

A few minutes later Malcolm Wainwright trotted down the hallway. He wore a faded *Mission U.K.* sweatshirt rolled up to the elbows, worn jeans and a pair of high-top sneakers. He was taller than O'Toole and looked trim and athletic, a basketball player or a runner. O'Toole had almost been expecting a mole, someone who spent his life inside the movie theater.

"Malcolm Wainwright," the man said, extending his hand. "Sorry to keep you waiting."

"Thanks for seeing me on such short notice." O'Toole said, standing up to shake hands.

After the introductions O'Toole began feeding him the story about looking for actresses and starlets.

"In search of ancient actresses, eh? I like that," Wainwright said. "It's a good peg for a piece. I'll tell you right now where they all are. The good actresses made it up to the regular features. The really good ones went over to Hollywood. Then the pretty ones, the girls who were more faces and figures than voices, well, if they were lucky, some of them married sugar-daddy oil execs, or politicians who kept them in styles they were unaccustomed to. Then again, there's a good number of them who are still making the slash-and-bash-and-burn-and-churn flicks. The poor bloody beautiful creatures.''

As he spoke with hardly any pause, Wainwright folded his arms across his chest. Though he was standing still, he seemed to be moving all the time, nodding his head with nervous energy.

O'Toole liked him, perhaps because he was an actual real writer but more because of his manner. Though energetic, Wainwright was relaxed and approachable when dealing with people, ready to help a friend. But then again, O'Toole didn't feel like much of a friend to anybody. He was merely doing his job. Since O'Toole was there under a false name and false pretense, he could only be a false friend.

They talked some more, then O'Toole took out the photocopy of Gabriella.

"Yeah, I know her," Wainwright said when he looked at the picture. "I mean I recognize her—I can't recall who she is yet. Give it time. She's been in lots of fantasies."

On-screen and off, O'Toole thought.

Wainwright stepped over to a long desk that held several bound volumes of film and shock magazines and started flipping through them. Wainwright was a one-man archive.

"Okay, Gabriella was the name you said. Right?"

"Gabriella and lots of other names, I guess." He rattled off a few of the names that Nanos had pried out of his junkie friend.

O'Toole stood next to him, watching page after glossy page of mayhem and debauchery flicker by as Wainwright riffled through the pages. It was a veritable history of horror, and screening it was the premiere historian of Britain.

As he searched through the volumes Wainwright said, "You've got to understand that everybody in these pictures used several different names, so the credits don't help much. Actors, directors, producers, distributors, they all used screen monikers. Sometimes they changed their names from film to film, other times they kept the same name for a whole string of movies. But then the movie titles changed just as often. Sometimes you could find the same movie showing under different names at the same time."

There were a few false starts, with Wainwright peering closer to examine one of the photographs, but then he would always pick up the pace again without saying anything.

Wainwright suddenly stopped flipping through the pages. "Ah, that could be her." He paused, rubbing his chin as he scanned the picture. "It's hard to tell though, with that ax in her head." He ran his fingers down a list of cast and credits, then said, "Okay, in this one it looks like she's going under the name of Laura Mansfield. If that's the same one, we'll be in luck..."

O'Toole waited patiently as Wainwright continued the search. The film writer had been working from the photocopy O'Toole had provided. Now that he had tentatively identified her, he could work from a more recent pose. Finally he stopped.

"I knew it. There she is ..."

As Wainwright rapped one of the glossy pages with his fingers, O'Toole peered over his shoulders and saw a girl in a black lace outfit holding a smoking Tommygun in her hands.

"That's it!" Wainwright said. "*Machine-gun Girls.* A great piece of bad work," he said.

O'Toole looked at the picture again. There was no doubt at all. The girl with the gun was Gabriella. She was going under the name of Laura Mansfield for the gun-moll flick.

Wainwright carefully removed the magazine with the picture of the actress and brought it over to a small photocopier. As he began making copies of the pages that listed actors, directors, and distributors, a strange look came over his face and his manner suddenly went cold. But he continued making copies, searching out different films that she appeared in so O'Toole would have a paper trail to follow.

He handed over a folder full of photocopies still warm to the touch. Then he stared O'Toole in the face. "I remember her pretty well now," Wainwright said. "She appeared in a lot of these movies, then suddenly vanished. Not another word from her for years."

O'Toole nodded.

"There is one more film she appeared in," Wainwright said. "It was a brand-new one. Just came out. But I didn't recognize her until now."

"What's that?" O'Toole said.

"The Shock Troupe movie," Wainwright said. He gave O'Toole an accusing stare. And though there was no doubt that O'Toole could take him apart, the film writer looked tempted to take a swing at him.

O'Toole half expected that. If Wainwright was a real media junkie, it was only natural that he'd pick up on the connection between the actress in the exploitation flick and the girl snuffed out for real.

"Yeah," O'Toole admitted. "She was in *Shock Troupe*."

Wainwright stood silent.

O'Toole waved the folder. "These might help me track down what happened to her. Let me pay you for your time."

"No," Wainwright said. Then, perhaps taking his cue from one of the countless film noir gangster epics he'd seen, he said, "You can do me a favor, though."

"What's that?"

"Just forget you ever saw me," Wainwright said.

O'Toole nodded. "If that's what you want." He waved the folder one more time. "Thanks."

"You do know she's dead now, don't you?" Wainwright asked.

"Yeah," O'Toole answered.

"Who the hell are you?"

"A fan," O'Toole said. "Just a fan." And in a way it was true. With his memory of the videotape still fresh, O'Toole felt like she was alive. But then again, if she were, he wouldn't be tracking down her killer.

8

"Roll camera," Derek Martin said, monitoring the house in the Cotswolds from a thickly wooded hillside across the road. He was scanning the area from left to right through the low-light scope mounted upon his rifle.

The house was surrounded by trees, a riotously blooming garden and a cadre of Shock Troupe soldiers.

More would be arriving any moment now. But first Martin had to set the scene.

They had previously captured some film of the two country dwellers from this very same spot, shooting in the daylight through unshuttered windows. It was the type of film that showed up in blue movies or was delivered in blank mailing wrappers to surprised statesmen who would shortly receive extortion calls.

Many of the statesmen would suddenly make a surprising about-face, taking a position they had previously campaigned against.

"Camera rolling," Thornton said. The assistant director zeroed in on the thatched-roof cottage that looked so serene in the first fall of evening.

Good contrast for what was to come, Martin thought.

The cottage was located at the apex of a bend in the road, and it was secluded by a waist-high wall of neatly piled stones.

Towering rows of luxurious oaks flanked it, and the upper part of the house was shaded by branches heavy with foliage. The shadows of the branches looked like spidery legs crawling over the roof.

"A man and his maid," Martin said, mocking the arrangement of the two inhabitants of the house below. One was an elderly British gentleman named Andrew Nesmith. The other was not very old at all. Denise Cadwaller was in her twenties and easily could have starred in one of Martin's exploitation films, if ever given the chance.

But she had made her choice long ago and was now living in it.

The small towns dotting the winding roads that cut through the forest were populated mostly by families who'd stayed there for generations, or those new-comers who were wealthy enough to purchase a sum-mer country home or a retreat for occasional dalliances.

Denise Cadwaller had lived here as a stranger, re-ceiving either cold looks from her neighbors or inter-ested, slightly mocking looks from the younger men who quite often made up reasons to visit while the older gentleman was away. And though there were a few she might have been interested in, she quickly shooed them off. She didn't want to complicate her life any further.

Derek Martin knew all there was to know about her and her esteemed lover.

Occupying the house in the sights of both gun and camera was a "retired" military man and his mistress, a would-be barrister who traded her ambitions for the amorous attentions of Andrew Nesmith. Nesmith kept her in comfort and company on those frequent occasions when he told his wife back in London that he had official business to take care of.

Life in the clandestine services had its perks. Andrew's wife was used to his sudden disappearances, those hush-hush assignments out of town that he couldn't speak about. All he could do was hint that the welfare of the country was at stake.

After all, he couldn't say that he was making sure to maintain his libido in a healthy state. In the decades he'd served his country as an officer in desert posts and regal embassies, he'd considered satisfying his needs of the utmost importance. It wouldn't do to have a high-strung man in the intelligence game.

At nine-thirty that evening Andrew Nesmith was incredibly low-strung, thanks to the frolicsome hours he'd spent with his brown-haired mistress.

If all went well, she would live and not one inch of her full-figured body would be hurt. In the interests of "justice," only the truly guilty would be attacked tonight.

Of course she would never live down the scandal. At best she would sell her story to the tabloids, the kind that featured cheery topless models on their inside page, playing the fallen woman to corrupt government man. Not only would she arouse the envy of the readers, but her story would portray Nesmith as an untrustworthy bugger who cheated on his wife—and maybe, with Shock Troupe "evidence," cheated on his country as well.

She would be left for the press to feed upon for a week or two of frenzy. Then she would sail off into oblivion, another discarded dream of the high and mighty.

The first part of the tragedy would be captured on film. Martin had the same crew with him as before. The assistant director, the stuntman and one of the few female operatives he could trust on a Shock Troupe operation. They would make their special guest appearance any moment now.

Like any director, he had prepared a couple of different endings for his "movie." In case things didn't work out the way he wanted, he had a sufficient back-up scenario for the hit. But he had little doubt it wouldn't go off as planned. They had cased the Cotswold hideaway and rehearsed their act well in advance of the showtime.

If not for the need for shock, along with the public relations value of sparing the girl, Martin could have taken the whole bloody house down with an RPG or two. That would have sent the fairy-tale life of the man from MI5 up in smoke.

But mistresses flash-fried into burning embers didn't look too good on camera.

Martin tracked the marble path from the front door to the access walkway in the stone wall. It was such an easy shot, such an unprotected sight, that it was almost criminal. All he had to do was to get Nesmith to come out of the cozy safety of his house and he had his man.

"ANOTHER?" Nesmith asked.

Denise Cadwaller shook her head *no*, both to the brandy proferred in his hand, and the sparkle in his eye that suggested renewed fun and games.

She was dressed in a white silky nightgown and was combing her long brown hair in front of the vanity mirror. Making herself look beautiful was perhaps the only skill that Nesmith credited her with.

"Well then," he said. "I'll take care of it for you." He set down his half-finished brandy on the table, then lined up hers right behind it.

It was good brandy. Nesmith felt he deserved the best in life. He knew where to get the best food, where to go for the best clothes, and who to go to for the best romance.

It was a perfect life. For him.

She was bored silly, hardly able to listen to him anymore. But he did provide for her, and that was a blessing of sorts.

Of course, she reminded herself at times, if she had continued her studies, maybe she could provide for herself. Ahh, she thought. What was the use? It was over and done with. Besides, she hadn't done so badly.

Lieutenant-Colonel Andrew Nesmith had "retired" from the Parachute Regiment in 1965. That much she knew. He then served in MI5, the Secret Intelligence Service. That much she guessed. He threw enough hints her way to let her know that he was an important man who, when he wasn't bedding her, was out keeping Britain safe.

He'd seen action in the Mideast, as she'd heard time and again during his stories about sultans he knew, about training their security people.

All in all he wasn't a bad man. He was just insufferably proud of himself. Especially of his abilities in bed.

Nesmith finished his brandy, then picked up hers. "Let's go downstairs and do a bit of listening," he said. The suggestion was more of an order. It was culture time, where they would sit facing one another, listening to an opera or other classical piece that she "must really get to know."

"Love to," she said.

MARTIN NODDED ONCE to his A.D. "Action," he said.

Thornton clicked twice on the small hand-held radio fastened to his belt, giving the cue to the remaining actors in the troupe who were waiting in their cars just a short distance away. He then focused on the front of the house. He'd catch more than that in the film, but the actors and their cars would be edited out. Except for the main actor in the spectacle.

The first Shock Troupe car came from the left. It was an old cream-colored Ford. The second car came from the opposite direction. It was a light gray station wagon stolen for its suburban good looks. Imitation wood panels gave it that homey touch that seemed to blend right in with the Cotswolds.

Adam Whitehouse drove the Ford. The broad-shouldered stunt man had the right amount of skill to carry off the act with the precision demanded.

The girl who drove the wagon, Gwen McCardle, was a black-haired siren who'd just about given up on becoming an actress when she was "discovered" by Derek Martin. He discovered her when she was reaching into his back pocket for his wallet inside a crowded nightclub.

Rather than hand her over to the police and condemn her to certain jail time because of previous offenses on her record, he turned her into a full-fledged member of Shock Troupe.

Martin weaned her from petty crime to high crime, bringing her along bit by bit. Whenever he felt she was ready for the next step, he gave her what she could handle, letting her taste more of the good life with each of her successes.

He'd found the anger in her and gave it a release.

Right now it was getting its release in the high speed of the station wagon as she tromped on the pedal. All she had to do was stomp on the brakes at the right time, more for the sound effect than anything else, and Whitehouse would take care of the rest.

Whitehouse reached the curve first. The stuntman took the turn wide, fishtailing the back of the car over the gravel at the side of the road before intentionally overcorrecting his skid and darting over to the wrong side of the road.

In case anyone was watching from the house, it looked like the actions of a garden variety maniac on the road. Drunk or reckless, it appeared real enough.

His car spun out, the back end swerving into the oncoming lane. The tire-burning skid forced the oncoming wagon to also cross lanes.

Gwen jerked the steering wheel hard, avoiding the crash with the other car. Her wagon shot off the road and careened into the stone walls in front of the cottage. Stones and slates went flying as the car smashed through the slender walkway.

Whitehouse hurtled out of his car and slammed the door behind him with a loud *Whump!* He swore at her in a strong Cockney accent, spitting out a steady stream of guttural curses.

Gwen staggered from her car, looking dazed as the huge man hurled abuse at her. "Leave me alone!" she shouted at the man who towered above, screaming with rage.

"Bloody fool bitch! I'm gonna knock some sense into your damn fool head."

She was standing on the marble path that led to Nesmith's house, raising her hand futilely to stop the quick blow coming her way.

His palm landed on her cheek with a loud slap, spinning her around.

The pain was real and ripped a shriek of agony from her lips. Blood coursed down her chin.

Gwen screamed for help as she stumbled toward the door of the cottage. She moved slowly as if she were in shock. Her eyes dazedly shifted focus from the brute slapping her to the sanctuary of the cottage.

His coarse shouts were loud enough to wake the dead, and certainly loud enough to reach the ears of Lieutenant-Colonel Andrew Nesmith.

The white-haired spook thundered through the front door in a pair of silk pajamas. He carried a gnarled walking stick that he waved around like a scepter.

"Stop!" he sputtered in anger, raising the cane over his head in a fit of righteous anger. "You barbarian. Let her be." He was caught up in the heroics and the need to sort things out. So caught up that he didn't listen to the inner voice telling him to slow down.

But he couldn't stop, not when the brute had grabbed the woman and was shaking her, totally ignoring Nesmith's protests.

Nesmith brought the stick down hard, and almost as if he'd anticipated it, counted on it, the brute moved out of the way.

Next the woman stepped in front of him, taking the blow of the walking stick on her shoulder.

For a moment Nesmith saw her heavily made-up face, and in a momentary impression it seemed to him that her hair was slightly askew in a stiff way, as if it were a wig.

She fell at his feet, raising her arm as if she was protecting herself from him and not the insane driver who'd been screaming at her a moment ago.

"What in hell is going on here?"

The combatants suddenly stood and backed away from him, the fire going out of their voices as if someone had just turned them off. They both acted as though the car accident had never happened, and regarded him calmly. Amusement danced in the girl's eyes, indifference in the man's.

Whitehouse and the girl stepped aside on opposite sides of the path. It all seemed choreographed now.

Neither one of them said a word. The Lieutenant-Colonel was struck dumb, too. Chivalry had propelled him out there, making him forget that any incident out of the ordinary, given what his profession was, had to be looked at with a wary eye.

Nesmith was still a muscular man. There was a lot of strength lying dormant beneath the bulk he'd accumulated over the years. He felt confident that he could handle one or both of the people in front of him. But Nesmith was intelligence man enough to know that the real threat wouldn't come from them.

It all happened in a fraction of a second. A lifetime of spycraft spelled it all out for him in a flash.

He glanced over his shoulder at the relative safety of the cottage but knew it might as well have been a hundred miles away. He was caught out in the open.

He looked back toward the two passive assailants, then beyond them at the hill across the road. His trained eyes picked out the spot an assassin would pick. Line of sight to the door. Good view to watch for anyone approaching.

Though he couldn't see anyone in the dark cluster of forest, a sixth sense told him someone was there.

Lieutenant-Colonel Andrew Nesmith raised his walking stick again, like a war club of old and shouted at his unseen enemy in the woods.

The first bullet *thypped* through his stomach, making him feel as if a knife was slicing through him. But the unbearable pain was eliminated by the next shot that pierced his heart.

His legs no longer worked, but his mind raced, trying to cram everything possible into that last moment as he fell down, as his back thumped onto the freshly mown grass.

The scent was good, welcoming. He could no longer see the man or the woman who had set him up, but he swung the walking stick, almost by reflex. He flung it in their direction as he went down. Before the stick hit the ground, he was dead.

His last thought was that at least he went out the way he wanted to. A soldier in battle.

"BEAUTIFUL," Derek Martin said.

The bullets that whacked Nesmith had planted gory seeds. A bloody mark blossomed on his chest like a huge scarlet letter. Perfect, if unanticipated symbolism, Martin thought. Sometimes the best art happened that way, unplanned but hatched into being with a primal design of its own.

He lowered the silenced sniper rifle. "That's a wrap," he said to Thornton.

He and the cameraman backed quickly up to the top of the hill, while the man and woman below piled into the Ford and drove off at high speed.

Later both cars would be found to have been stolen.

So would the car waiting for Martin and Thornton on the other side of the woods, the car that would speed him to the premiere of the opening scene of another Shock Troupe production.

9

Two hours after the assassination, Derek Martin drove up the winding road to his King's Glen estate. He was riding in a Bentley, having changed cars along the way. On the seat beside him was the videotape of the latest Shock Troupe performance.

Martin was alone now that the shoot had gone well.

The assistant director had been given the task of ditching the stolen cars, planting misleading information in them to throw any investigation off the track and then seeing to the getaway of the Shock Troupe actors.

It was like a real movie. Everyone had their assigned roles.

Martin swung the car to the top of the circular drive. A number of other cars were parked alongside, most of them expensive late models.

Owned by Martin's production company, the cars were predominantly black and gray, the uniform colors of the British establishment men who were so often ferried in them, accompanied behind the dark-curtained windows by gaily laughing women.

Lights glowed from just a few of the windows in the house, giving it a somewhat somber and abandoned look. It made him feel tired, but he couldn't sleep yet. He had more work to do.

Once in the house, Martin hurried to the kitchen, which was equipped with an outsized hearth as tall as a man. It was a survivor of the days when the house had to feed an army of servants, guards and guests.

Now it served a smaller army.

Martin popped a couple of Dexedrines into his mouth. It was a habit left over from his days of politics and rage. Although he'd seen others turn paranoid or manic from Dexedrine boosts, he was sure he could handle it.

Besides, he no longer washed them down with cheap wine or champagne, the way he did when he was younger. Now a wiser man, he washed them down with water.

Hoping the stimulants would kick in soon—it was well past midnight—Martin headed down the long corridor that led to the underground rooms.

While the upper floors of the house maintained the old glamour and were decked out in traditional fashion, the floors below were modern soundproof production rooms or movie stages.

Art deco dungeons, one of his actresses had called them.

The largest room was known as the War Room. It also doubled as the conference room for the inner circle of Shock Troupe members.

Martin carried the videotape they'd just filmed down to the War Room, flicking on the lights as soon as he entered. Subdued lighting glowed onto a long console of video monitors.

It was the director's throne room.

Plush chairs on rollers sat in front of each monitor. The chairs had to be comfortable. It took hours of editing and crosscutting to create a successful film.

He felt at ease in the War Room. It suited his personality. It was actually a movie set Martin had used several times in the past. Whenever he needed to shoot scenes with a military setting, this was where he staged them.

Here square-jawed officers of the cinema could come in and plan their campaigns against invasions of giant bugs, lizards, or sixty-foot-tall women with Everest-sized breasts. It was also used for a science fiction parody he'd done where Space Patrol generals gathered to scratch their heads in wonder. The running joke throughout the film had the generals wondering if the two-headed alien ambassadors really wanted world peace or were just talking out of both sides of their mouths.

Cheap celluloid fantasies like that had made him a fortune, putting him in a spot where he could turn his dreams into realities. Although the Shock Troupe episodes were much harder and more dangerous to carry out, the rewards were a world apart.

With Shock Troupe productions he could temporarily move beyond the level where he made movies about different worlds, and into a sphere where he could actually make the world different from before.

Derek walked over to the middle of three blackboards positioned end-to-end on the wall in front of the video consoles. He raised the shutter of the blackboard, revealing a gallery of photographs, maps and timetables.

From the chalk tray he picked up a pen-sized metal pointer and pressed the release button. The compressed pointer flicked out like a stiletto, telescoping into the feet of metal with a blunt round tip.

Whack.

He slashed the pointer into a blown-up photograph of a man in uniform. A jagged scar erupted on the glossy face as the ripped paper curled up. It was a diagonal cut that severed the right side of the man's face, running up from his neck to the end of his jawbone.

Martin whipped the pointer one more time, his sense of balance demanding a more realistic cut. This time the pointer slashed across the man's chest.

The director grabbed the shredded photograph of Andrew Nesmith and tore if off the blackboard. Then he crumpled it up into a ball and tossed it into the wastebasket.

"Bravo, Lieutenant-Colonel," he said. "You'll be a hard act to follow."

Martin stepped back and looked at the parts of the world he yet had to change.

There were other photographs of men and women of various nationalities. Several military installations around Britain were pinpointed on a map. Included on the board were targets of opportunity as well as planned Shock Troupe attacks.

"Coming soon to a theater near you," Martin said. He had more planning to do for the next Shock Troupe attack, but first he had to add the final touches to the tape of Andrew Nesmith.

Martin dropped into his seat behind the console, then slid the chair forward. He slapped the master tape in the video deck on top of the console to his left, then turned on a triple-tier column of decks below the console on his right.

The top deck had a blank tape that would take feeds from the master tape and the middle deck. The middle deck held a videotape of war atrocities that he'd ordered Thomas Crowell to compile from the massive footage the newsman could access at the INS building.

Then there was the bottom deck which had a tape of the rather X-rated scenes they'd already shot of Nesmith and his mistress.

With Martin's magic touch, the final tape would have the perfect blend of villainy and outrage, painting Nesmith as a creature that had to be destroyed.

He ran the Shock Troupe tape first, scanning that night's hit. It had come out well. There was plenty of footage of Nesmith swinging his cane and of Gwen getting hit. He might use it to portray Nesmith as a woman beater if it could fit in well with the rest of the footage. Then there were the primary shots—the footage of the Lieutenant-Colonel getting ripped by two bullets.

The scarlet letter looked beautiful.

Martin wouldn't show Nesmith lying on the ground for too long. No sense in letting the audience build up sympathy for the villain.

He rewound the Nesmith tape, then turned on the prepared tape of war atrocities.

On-screen came a desolate scene of massacred villagers. It was a small town in Yemen where the entire population had been murdered and were laid around their huts like stacks of kindling. The fact that the massacre had been carried out by Yemini rebels was considered irrelevant by Martin.

Nesmith had served there. The record would show that he was involved in counterinsurgency. That would let the audience read between the lines. Plus there were the other atrocities Martin would edit in. He had selected footage of massacres, executions and tortures, from every area where Nesmith had been stationed.

He had served with distinction as advisor or combatant in Malaya, Oman, and Yemen. Distinctions that would be artfully blurred by Derek Martin. All those gruesome scenes falsely attributed to the British soldier would be followed by the payoff scene—the Shock Troupe execution of Lieutenant-Colonel Andrew Nesmith.

He lost himself in the process, splicing bits and pieces of the tapes together until he'd doctored reality enough to come up with another Shock Troupe "document."

Martin pushed himself away from the console. The chair rolled across the soft carpeting.

His mind was racing. Although his work on the tape was finished, he didn't want to stop. The Dexedrine boosters had picked him up and were ready to carry him around for the rest of the night.

Sleep was out for the next couple of hours at least, and he decided to turn his attention to the next Shock Troupe action.

It couldn't hurt to rehearse again, especially since he was using another group of actors to help Shock Troupe out.

This time he would be assisted by "The Hessians," as he called his auxiliary troops.

Martin had no doubts about the ability of *his* private troupe to carry out the riskier assignments. Either they would succeed or die trying—even if he had to kill them in the process. He never left anyone behind who could lead the enemy to him.

It was the Hessians he was bringing in that concerned him, the mercs from Hamburg. Led by a former French Legionnaire who'd plied his trade in southeast Africa, they were reliable but a bit too wild for his taste.

But then again, assassins didn't come made to order.

Martin would have preferred to rely solely on his own followers but he was limited. If he recruited too many people, sooner or later one of them would make the fatal mistake that would lead the enemy to him.

Rather than dilute the power of Shock Troupe by spreading them too thin, it made sense to bring in some additional firepower from time to time.

Like most underground power brokers, he had access to free-lance armies composed of troops who didn't mind what they did or whom they had to do it to. As long as the money was there, they were like attack dogs, killers with no allegiance to a cause that wouldn't fit into their wallet.

Right now the hired hit team was living out their covers as gentlemen farmers at a place in the New Forest area that Martin had leased through a number of cutouts.

Only one or two of the "farmers" were visible at a time, the rest of them staying hidden inside the huge farmhouse. They were mostly Germans, some with

Foreign Legion experience, some with experience from South Africa.

But a few of them could speak English.

Martin smiled, remembering his earlier conversation with their leader, the innocent-looking but homicidal Kruge. When told of the need for English-speaking troops, he'd tried to get more money from Martin.

"You should be able to speak Martian for the money we're paying you," Martin had said.

The merc shrugged. "Just a thought."

"I'm not paying you for thoughts," Martin said. "I'm paying you for action."

Martin went over his plan for the Germans once again, mentally rehearsing every aspect of the upcoming hit. Coming hard on the heels of the Nesmith assassination, it would tax the Brits beyond belief, making them throw logic out the window. They wouldn't know what hit them or who or how.

Martin thought of the mercs. While he was staying up half the night taking care of the minute details, they were probably asleep, perhaps even passed out from drink.

Of course he'd know soon enough.

Martin usually had one of his men scout the area at random to check up on the hired help.

10

The England of idyllic countryside that most people maintained in their imagination was mostly an illusion.

The real exception was the New Forest Region.

While much of the country had become gray and bleak by industry and overcrowding, in the south of England the wilds had been kept intact.

Small and wild New Forest ponies still roamed freely through the woods, and the deer herd was nearly as thick as it was a thousand years ago. At one time a royal forest and hunting preserve for the nobility, New Forest had become a refuge for those still looking for pastoral England.

Abbey ruins were peacefully crumbling beneath towering oaks and black spruce trees. Villages had sprung up around the perimeters while keeping the central wilderness intact. More than a hundred square miles of forest were ringed by hamlets, farms and lodges.

The environment afforded an idyllic existence— even for the German mercenaries encamped at a farm on the edge of New Forest.

The closest village was miles away at Mockbeggar. The farm was screened by woods on all sides, and access was gained by a long dirt road bordered by picket fences.

It was a good place to lie low until they were called into action, and the southern coast of England wasn't far away in the event they had to make a run for it. Still, they were anxious to get on with the job and get it behind them.

THE SAS KILLGROUNDS at Hereford hosted six Americans throughout the morning and into the afternoon.

They were guests of Brendan Laird, who shepherded them through the grounds with a minimum of contact with any of the other special teams familiarizing themselves with weapons or practicing assaults on mock-up targets.

Most of the weapons were Heckler & Koch, one of the premier designers for special forces. They had proven their worth several times over in SAS operations.

SAS had their own designers dreaming up weapons, but so far most of their specially produced equipment was in the surveillance and assault logistics area.

A high-tech group of SAS men known as the Ops Research Team had developed a wide array of monitoring equipment that included drop-down microphones to eavesdrop through chimneys and the "silenced" rubber-coated assault ladders that let their men get into position undetected to employ the mikes.

The SAS Ops Team also used thermal imagers and other night optic devices to provide as complete a picture of their assault target as possible. The picture was then given to the action team going in on the operation.

But in the case of the SOBs, they provided the picture. It was a totally black operation, and officially the SOBs hadn't even gone to Hereford nor had they received any intelligence.

It wasn't too hard to cover the tracks. Along with Brendan Laird's normal discretion, there was one more thing riding in his favor.

Officially the SOBs didn't exist, even in their own country.

LEE HATTON strapped herself into the white protective vest, glancing in the long barracks mirror to see that it properly shielded her chest and back. Barrabas stood beside her, helping her slip armor plates into the contoured vest.

Subdued sparks jumped between them as his hands brushed against her skin, but the moment passed quickly. Neither of them could afford any distractions that night.

"You look great," Barrabas said. "For a linebacker."

"Right," she said. "Or maybe a big-time wrestler."

The other SOBs were already geared up, waiting outside in one of the customized British Leyland Range Rovers that Jessup had obtained for them earlier.

Barrabas and Hatton had been the last ones in from the course and the last ones to shower up.

"We really need all this?" Lee asked, patting the armor plates that weighted down her vest.

"If we don't," Barrabas said, "all we'll lose is a bit of sweat." He paused before strapping on his vest, looking at the jagged scar tissue that streaked up from his collarbone and raced across his shoulder muscle, one of many souvenirs from his tours of duty with the SOBs. "But if we do need protection tonight and don't wear these...then we won't know what hit us and it won't matter."

Without plates the vests could take hits from a 9 mm submachine gun. With plates, the wearer could also survive a direct hit from a 7.62 NATO round.

"Just the same, we need speed to do this right," Hatton said. "And this will slow us down."

"Lead slows you down even more," Barrabas said. "No one likes wearing body armor—until they get hit by the first slug." Barrabas knew what he was talking about. Getting hit dead-on in the chest with a bullet and then walking around still able to fight...now that was a supernatural sensation, almost a religious experience, Barrabas thought.

Hatton shrugged. It wasn't an issue. On another day she would have been giving the same lecture. The complaint wasn't real, just something convenient to blow away the tension building up inside her.

The SOBs had been on hold ever since they'd arrived. True, there were some leads, like the one that Nanos and O'Toole had dug up that perhaps promised to uncover some of the slain actress's past. But that would take a while to pan out and involved more patience, watching and digging.

Tonight at last they'd been given the green light. Switched on.

Barrabas finished outfitting his armor, then followed Hatton outside.

Claude Hayes was driving their Rover. He looked relaxed, as if he'd spent a day at the races instead of jumping through the hurdles himself. Then again, Hayes always made it a point to look relaxed no matter what was going down.

O'Toole, Nanos and Billy Two were in the second Rover, with Nanos telling the other SOBs about the purple-haired girl in Piccadilly who wanted to pay *him* for his time.

Both of the customized Rovers were painted in civilian colors looking like the upscale versions favored by so many celebrities and woodsmen, and the passengers appearance was casual, too.

The clean-cut SOBs were dressed in civilian clothes. War-paint would come later, since for the time being it served their purposes better to look as though they were going on holiday.

It would, however, be an excursion out of the ordinary daily existence as known by most people. And the equipment for the unusual outing—special weaponry and other devices—was ready and waiting under a canvas covering.

THE WOODS WERE ALIVE when Whitehouse woke. Something was moving around, otherwise he wouldn't have stirred from the sleep he'd fallen into.

The Shock Troupe stuntman had attuned himself to the sounds of the forest at night while he'd been watching the farmhouse below. His subconscious could accept the sounds of the sudden rush of dark wings in flight or the scrambling of tiny claws in the underbrush.

What had woken him, then? Whitehouse felt a cold shadow of fear creep up his spine.

He was hidden in absolute darkness. Thick boughs swaying overhead blanketed him from the moonlight. That was what had made him fall asleep in the first place. He had felt secure until now. There was nothing for him to fear because *he* was the marauder.

It was his job to watch the mercs down there and make sure they were prepared and available when the time came. Martin might have to call them into action at any moment, and he had indicated the coming events were crucial in his strategy.

They had two large hits to carry out, and Martin wanted the hired soldiers in prime fighting condition. Most definitely, he didn't want them attracting undue attention to themselves.

Whitehouse had no illusions about his abilities. If the mercenaries were on the rampage by any chance and he were to become their victim, there was no way he could stop them all. They could easily tear him apart.

Whitehouse could dispatch one individual. He'd done that several times in the past, but he'd always had the advantage of distance or sudden ambush.

But in a close fight, the mercs would shred him to pieces. It was a matter of degree: Whitehouse was an assassin, but those men down there were killers. His job was to report back to his field commander. Derek Martin would take care of the rest.

He'd leave out the part about falling asleep in his report. His orders had been to sit tight on the mercs and make sure they'd stayed on their leash until Martin sent them into action. He hadn't been ordered to dream away the night.

Though he was hidden well, he had a solid vantage point of the farmhouse. He stayed immobile for a time, hoping to see whoever was gliding nearly soundlessly through the woods.

The sounds that reached him were little more than the sound of breezes rustling through the branches. Almost natural sounds. If he'd been awake when he first heard them, they might not have disturbed him, because they were so close to the natural sound of the forest.

But the subconscious was a better guardian, and his instinct for self-preservation had told him to stir from the light sleep.

He moved slowly, fanning out his fingertips as he stretched his hands. Then he cautiously and silently reached for his holster and lifted the flap.

Whitehouse sat up inch by inch and moved his head about with the patience of a sloth. He scanned the immediate forest through the fallen brush he'd gathered around him.

Sitting in a sunken pocket of earth that was flanked by a pair of intertwined oaks, he felt like a nocturnal animal timidly poking his head out to see what was on the prowl. Whitehouse picked up the low-light Pilkington Pocketscope and brought it to his right eye. He continued sweeping left to right, raising and lowering it with the contours of the woods.

Suddenly he saw his first ghost. It showed up on the passive night-vision device as a man-sized specter, then it dropped out of sight.

There were a lot of drop-offs and ravines in the woods, making it impossible for him to fully track the spot unless he physically went after him.

The cool spring air had suddenly turned icy, reflecting his internal emotional temperature. One of the mercs going out on patrol? he wondered. It was possible. But he would imagine them to have sentries closer to the farm property, rather than moving purposefully through the forest.

Whitehouse lowered the scope. In its place he unholstered his Browning Hi-Power autoloader with a thirteen-round magazine.

The woods seemed to be moving again, with minute signs of a starting and stopping process. The sound seemed to parallel his own breathing. But it came in a slower and steadier rhythm, the breathing of predators.

Off to his right the brush shook slightly, and a faint hissing sound reached him like the forest exhaling its breath. Then a footfall sounded on hard earth. Man, not animal, was walking behind him.

More sound came from another location, like the wind hurrying through the woods.

How many are there? he thought.

He lowered his pistol and sank back into the pocket of earth. He wasn't about to shoot—not when there were so many shapes moving about in the night.

For a moment Whitehouse felt as though he was in a haunted hollow of woods. The spooks had claimed New Forest as their own.

He was the intruder, not them.

Whitehouse shivered. The bed of dirt he'd carved out for himself had been damp and cold before. Now it promised to become his deathbed.

What the hell was he doing here? What had Martin got him into?

Until now no one had really entered the field they'd fought on. Shock Troupe came in hard, made their hit, then got out. They always had the advantage of surprise.

But to have someone looking for him, actually scouring the woods...

Whitehouse forced himself to breathe slowly to calm down the raging blood that pounded away inside of him. It beat in his heart like loud footsteps running in wild circles. It coursed through his veins like rapids taking him over a gaping chasm. The sound of his own blood running in panic was louder to him than the rustling of the mysterious force through the trees.

Then more footsteps sliced through the forest, followed by just a brief burst of wind, then nothing.

The hunters were good. They wouldn't be caught all at once. Some were ahead on point, and some were behind, hanging back just enough to come to the forward man's aid.

He'd report back to Martin that there were at least a dozen, maybe more. There had to be that many to go after the mercs in the farmhouse. Because he'd understood that to be the drift of the circumstances.

He was getting out, he decided. He was just a stuntman. He was a trouper, not a one-man army. Those kind of dramatics only happened in the silly-ass movies that Martin made to bring in funds for his operations.

Whitehouse lifted the night scope again and swept the area for the enemy.

Through the foliage he saw the shapes moving in and out of range, never staying long in one spot, never presenting good targets. And they were traveling fast, much faster than he thought possible for the minute sounds they were making.

He started to turn around when, from close quarters, he heard something that couldn't quite be called a sound. It was off to his right. He swore he could almost hear breathing.

Whitehouse froze. Any trace of the predator about him vanished and burrowed down into the cold earth like a spirit leaving his body. His moment of truth came. He knew who he was now. But could he live with that. The problem was that unless he was very careful, he could die with that.

Adam Whitehouse had just toppled from the hierarchy of the jungle. Instead of one of the superior beasts, one of the hunters, he realized that he was just one more creature in the chain. The real hunters of the night were prowling all around him.

He lowered the scope and dropped back into his cocoon.

NILE BARRABAS WAS the forward point of a 7.62 mm triangle.

Claude Hayes and Liam O'Toole formed the left and right corners of the triangle. Each of them was buried in the brush, armed with a modified sound-suppressed sniper rifle. The Heckler & Koch *Prazisionsschutzengewehrs* were blackened so that no glint of moonlight would give them away.

Like the other SOBs, Nile's face was smeared with dark green camo paint, and his clothes were uniformly black, the nightmare colors of the SAS.

Barrabas scoped the front of the farmhouse. Through the windows he could see Kruge sitting at a long wooden table, a bottle of whiskey beside him, cards in front of him.

The SOB chieftain held him in the crosshairs for a moment, then tracked down the faces of the other mercs gathered around the table.

The ones he couldn't see were covered by Hayes and O'Toole, who were focusing on other farmhouse windows with their sniper scopes.

Barrabas tracked back down the far side of the table, settling the crosshairs once more on Kruge who sat at the head of the table like the patriarch of a clan. It was a killing clan, however. Kruge's bunch specialized in kidnappings, bank robberies, art heists and outright murder.

The most recent outrage credited to the German mercenary was the kidnapping of a Belgian family, heirs to a weapons manufacturer. Having convinced the family's negotiators to avoid the police, he'd ransomed the entire family for a large consignment of factory-fresh weaponry and a considerable chunk of cash. After the ransom was transferred to Kruge, he released them as promised, letting them drive off in a large sedan.

But it was customized. As soon as the car reached the waiting negotiators Kruge pressed a small button on the remote control unit. The plastic explosive strips planted throughout the car were detonated, turning the man, his wife and three children into rockets of flesh and bone ripping through the roof. The explosion also took out a couple of the family retainers who'd been handling the negotiations.

Kruge's assignment had been to assassinate the weapons heir. But rather than let the opportunity go to waste, he'd demanded the ransom of weapons and money on his own. He always did the job, but on his own terms.

Kruge was a wild card, but he was about to be aced.

The others were scattered around the table, smoking, drinking, and playing cards. Going out of their minds with boredom.

The SOBs would soon alleviate that boredom, though none of the mercs would be grateful.

BILLY TWO silently and invisibly approached the sentry who'd been leaning against a weathered support pole.

The man was in the shelter of an overgrown lean-to, which provided a roof over an old hay wagon long out of use. Covered by the slanting overhang of the roof, the sentry was well shadowed. He kept a sleepy eye on the access road, expecting any trouble to come from there. But the SOBs weren't about to announce themselves at the front gate. Trouble came to the sentry from the woods to his left in the form of the Osage Indian who was perfectly at home in any kind of darkness and any kind of wilderness.

Billy Two stepped softly through the overgrown grass, lifting his feet easily and placing them down firmly, rather than sliding through the grass.

He was silent, and he was in war paint. And he was perfectly at home.

The mercenary sentry was good. He sensed danger moving in on him. It wasn't visually that he was tipped off but his sixth sense. Death had come finally, after stalking him for decades across several continents.

Billy Two rushed forward.

The mercenary tried to bring his weapon to bear on the attacker but wasted a vital moment getting his balance. To be comfortable during his watch he'd been leaning back with his head resting against the pole. His feet were planted at an angle that made him incapable of immediate response.

Billy Two lashed out with his right forearm. It caught the sentry in the neck, and the force of the strike pressed him back against the wooden pillar. His feet were lifted off the ground briefly by the shock that streamed through his body. Simultaneously with the forearm strike, Billy Two tugged at the man's weapon and ripped it out of his hands. He tossed it silently into the tall grass.

Curling his hand around the back of the man's neck, he next dealt a blow to the head and swept the silenced sentry to the ground.

Lee Hatton and Alex Nanos moved from the shadows and followed Billy Two toward the house. The trio quickly took up prearranged positions around the farmhouse, preparing to use their flash-bang stun grenades, tear gas canisters and plastic explosive strips.

They were armed with Heckler & Kock MP5SDs, silenced submachine guns outfitted with a laser-lock system that showed where the stream of bullets was going to flow. In the right hands, the MP5 could result in virtually instant hits without having to aim through the sights. The SMG could be shot from the hip with total accuracy. All that had to be done was to follow the red laser dot, then squeeze the trigger.

One more figure stepped from the woods, hanging back near the edge. Brendan Laird was present as backup and observer. Barrabas had assigned him a position on the left side of the farmhouse.

Nile didn't particularly like the setup. Laird wanted to come in with the SAS Counter Revolutionary Warfare back-up team that had flown down to the area with him by helicopter hours ago. But Barrabas turned down the CRW unit.

"I figured on six people for this operation, counting myself," Barrabas had said. "I can handle seven, counting you as an observer. But I'll tell you right now, anyone else crashes this party, they might go down for keeps."

Laird studied him long enough to see that his stand was absolute. Barrabas had accepted his presence, but that was the limit.

"You got anyone else on the scene, you keep 'em back," Barrabas said. "And don't call in any air cavalry you've got on standby until I say so. Otherwise, tonight's *show* is canceled. We understand each other?"

Laird noted the stress on the word show. Barrabas had figured out a lot more than the logistics of the hit, he'd figured out the why of it. And he also knew about SAS strike methods in the country.

Choppers would come in out of nowhere to hop-scotch SAS teams to roadblocks or ambush sites. After seeding the field with commandos, they'd leave the area until the hunt was over or they were called back.

"It's your show," Laird agreed.

"That it is," Barrabas said. "Big show, small audience. And you've got the ringside seat."

The SAS liaison nodded.

"Nothing personal," Barrabas said. "These are my people. They're used to my ways."

The SAS man had filtered into the woods then.

There was no way of avoiding his presence. True, the SOBs were here to handle the matter. Intelligence indicated that the merc team was planning a double play—a strike on Russians, and then Americans.

Since it was on English soil they weren't going to give the SOBs carte blanche. Even black operations that didn't exist had their chain of command, and it was only natural that they have an observer along, even if that observer was armed to the teeth.

Barrabas had kept his Heckler & Koch PSG1 trained on the farmhouse while the SOB assault team took up their positions. Hayes and O'Toole, the other members of the sharpshooter team maintained the same quiet vigil. They flanked Barrabas on either side, far enough away so they had a wide kill-range, but close enough to stay within hearing.

The sniper rifles were like extensions of their body. They'd spent a lot of time at the Hereford range adjusting the rifles and practicing marksmanship at a variety of light levels. The battery-powered illumination of the 6 x 42 Hensoldt Wetzler scope had more than enough range for them to ID their targets.

To avoid any confusion, they'd selected their targets beforehand, assigning numbers to each. Norbert Kruge had been designated as "Number One."

Right now his number was up.

As he sat at the table, Kruge looked more like a successful accountant than a mercenary leader. He was slim, but not slight. His body was pared down to the essentials. He struck fast, hard and mean. There was more than enough graves throughout Europe to testify to that.

And he did have a head for figures. In fact, pyramiding his deals to squeeze out every last cent was what made him tick. He'd made several fast fortunes and lost them just as quickly.

But one thing was certain for Norbert Kruge. There was always more at one of the "banks," as he called the underground cells that funded operators like him. He was in demand. Not only could he take out his targets, but if it was necessary to make a big splash, he wasn't wary of shedding blood.

"Let's call 'em out," Barrabas said, in a low voice that became inaudible quickly, as stirring sounds made by the wind muffled it. He started the procedure himself. "Number One sighted," he said, focusing on the upper right corner of the window.

"Two sighted," Hayes said.

"Three sighted," O'Toole answered.

With all three men locked ono their primary targets, Barrabas gave the "kill" order.

He squeezed off the first round.

The 7.62 mm NATO slug punched through the windowpane, then zipped right through Norbert Kruge. It caught him in the right shoulder, then knocked him back out of the chair.

Despite the kill order, Barrabas wasn't trying to eliminate the mercenary leader. There was a chance he might provide direct leads to Shock Troupe people.

Hayes and O'Toole opened up on both sides, their rounds crashing through windows, aimed at the startled mercs who tumbled back from the table unaware they'd been dealt their last hands.

Barrabas continued firing, progressing from right to left down the table. Designed for accurate and rapid fire, the sniper rifles each held a twenty-round magazine.

They laid down enough fire for a small army.

BILLY TWO DETONATED the explosive strips planted at the front and back doors of the house. His signal had been the first bullet the sniper team dispatched through the window.

As the startled mercs inside the house got to their feet, they would instinctively head for the doors—doors that were now blowing inward.

Nanos and Hatton launched flash-bangs into the farmhouse at the same time, and saw one of the mercs smash through a side window while behind him the white hell of the stun grenades lit up the interior. He had a stranglehold on a Czech Skorpion machine pistol that was already spitting lead as he flew in the air. He tumbled and rolled, still firing toward the front of the house.

Lee Hatton followed his progress with the laser dot, then let it rip with a three-round burst.

Whap-whap-whap.

He kept on rolling, but no longer of his own power. The slugs had knocked him off balance, carrying him to his last destination, a fragile bush of dry branches that cracked beneath his dead weight.

The three black-clad SOBs strafed the windows and open doorways, sweeping the stunned mercs to the floor.

Billy Two was standing to the right of the doorway when one of the mercs came running out, screaming in German that he wanted to surrender.

The German looked like he was wearing war paint, but the stripes were streaks of blood running down his face. He ran right up to Billy Two.

The Osage cracked his jaw with a ham fist that sent the would-be prisoner reeling. He followed up with a kick to the ribs that would keep him down for a while and make sure that he didn't change his mind.

Nanos lifted his knee into another one wanting to surrender. He thumped his back with an elbow strike that planted him on the ground.

There was no time for niceties. Surrender was risky at best in the middle of a firefight, especially when, suddenly, automatic fire opened up on them from the second floor.

Hatton flicked to full-auto and sprayed the upper-floor windows.

A moment later more fire spit out, the slugs chewing into the ground near Lee Hatton. She rolled for cover and slapped in another clip.

It had taken about a minute since the beginning of the assault, and some of the mercs had gathered their wits and were making a stand on the second story.

Lee swiveled to her left when she saw another shadow moving by the side of the house, but she held her fire. It was Brendan Laird.

While the mercs were occupied with their firefight, he'd swung a black cable with a grappling hook up to the second floor, relying on the heavy gunfire to cover the sound of the hook as it caught on the chimney.

He was rapidly climbing up to the second floor, his feet hardly making any noise.

Lee put out covering fire to distract the top-floor gunners.

Billy Two moved toward the back of the house, firing sporadically at the second floor.

Nanos took up a position behind and to the right of Lee Hatton. Whenever one of the gunners fixed on Hatton and fired from one of the windows, Nanos drove them back with a full-auto burst.

The SAS man crept onto the roof. He moved soundlessly to the dormer where the mercs had last fired from. Then he waited, listening for the voices inside.

The SOBs held their fire.

Laird balanced himself on the slanting roof, moving hand over hand down the eaves of the dormer.

He paused as if he were filling his lungs before diving into water. After breathing deeply and exhaling softly, he dived through the already shattered window, pushing through the sundered wood and splinters of glass.

Two wounded mercs were too surprised at an apparition at such close quarters to react quickly.

But Laird was already firing. His first burst stitched the closest merc across the chest, sending his carcass thumping back into the remaining merc. Laird continued moving. While the last merc scrambled for a shot, the SAS man doubled him over with a three-round burst that tumbled him to the floor.

BARRABAS, O'TOOLE and Hayes approached the house and were ready to open fire when the others gave the all clear.

Nanos had herded the prisoners to the side of the house, where they were lying facedown. Their hands were tied behind their necks while they ate dirt.

Leaving O'Toole and Hayes outside to patrol the area, Barrabas stepped inside.

Smoke and dust, shattered wood, and the odor of freshly spilled blood swirled around the room. It looked like an armory and a cemetery combined. Overturned chairs stayed propped up like tombstones over the fallen mercs. Hatton was attending to one of the wounded who was sitting in the corner, groaning, spitting out everything he knew in German.

Billy Two filled Barrabas in on the number of survivors. Kruge was dead. He'd caught a second burst from the Osage in the early stages of the battle. It couldn't be helped. Rather than reason with the wounded but gun-wielding German, Billy Two had cut him down.

Hatton filled Barrabas in on Laird's actions.

"I know," Barrabas said. "I saw it go down." He'd used the night-vision scope to watch the progress of the battle, now and then squeezing off rounds to protect the flanks of the SOB assault team.

Barrabas turned to their SAS contact. "Nice work," he said. "Where'd you learn to observe like that?"

Laird shrugged. "They had to be taken out," he said. "I was available."

"Thanks," he said. "But we have to talk. And soon." He made arrangements to sit down with Laird and go over any intelligence the house or the survivors yielded. The prisoners were all wanted by various European agencies and would cut any deals they could.

"We did what we came for," Barrabas said. "Hope you liked the show. Now call in your people."

Laird nodded.

Shortly afterward the air was split by a siren. Emergency rescue vehicles. Medevacs. Police and intelligence teams were descending on the area.

By the time they reached the spot, the SOBs would be gone.

"How's this going down in the media?" Barrabas asked.

Laird surveyed the surroundings, then looked back at Barrabas. "If you ask me, it appears that gangland factions had a shootout in the English countryside."

11

Adam Whitehouse drove straight to King's Glen manor. He forced himself to keep well within the speed limit, to avoid being noticed by the police.

By the time he arrived, one of Martin's late-night soirees was winding down. Strains of music and laughter escaped from the brightly lighted windows and floated out onto the grand expanse of lawn.

The stuntman had changed into the spare jeans and jacket he kept in the car and brushed himself off as much as possible. But he was still grimy from his vigil in the woods. No change of clothing could cover that up.

In his condition, Whitehouse would attract too much attention using the main entrance, although many of the rowdy and drunken guests probably wouldn't notice if he charged in on horseback. Still, Martin would have his head if he didn't show discretion.

He was in for it, anyway, judging from the ice that had been in his voice when Whitehead called earlier to warn that he was coming with bad news.

Whitehouse used the supply entrance at the back of the manor, then made his way undetected to the host's private quarters. He rapped on the closed door, then announced himself.

"Come in, by all means," Martin said, and White-house swung the door inward. He stopped midway through the open door when he saw that Martin had company.

Deborah Quarry, the actress Whitehouse had pursued in his serpent costume, had been captured. But her captor was Derek Martin.

She was sitting on the edge of the bed. Her evening dress was tossed over a chair back.

"You know my guest," Martin said.

"Yes, of course," Whitehouse said. "Good evening. I'm sorry to interrupt..."

He found himself staring at her.

Both straps of her chemise had drifted down her shoulders. The lacy black silk contrasted sharply with her milky-white skin. Though he'd seen her in less, now the lacy black straps seemed like borders of pleasure marking forbidden territory. At least for him.

Her long hair was gathered into a thick braid that ran down her back like a whip. Her presence made his sojourn in the woods seem like cruel and unusual punishment. While he was risking life and limb in a forest full of berserk commandos, Martin was sitting warm and cozy—with a starlet for a companion.

Martin noticed his hungry gaze with amusement. "Deborah, I think you're too distracting. If you could leave us for a while?" Like most of the suggestions Martin made these past few days, it was an order.

The B-movie queen leaned over and grabbed her dress. Her eyes taunted Whitehouse as she slithered into it and then slipped out of the room.

Martin's smile disintegrated the moment she closed the door behind her. "What happened to our friends?" Martin asked.

"They were hit by a team of commandos."

"How many?"

"I don't know," the stuntman said. "I couldn't see them all. They moved quick. But the way they took that place apart, they had to be a small army."

"And you just sat and watched," Martin said. His narrow visage seemed like an ax about to strike.

Whitehouse quickly explained what he'd observed of the commandos and their tactics, coloring the situation in his favor. He'd seen what happened to others who offended Martin's sense of artistry, whether it was in films or actual Shock Troupe operations.

"I had no choice," Whitehouse said. "If I wanted to get back alive—"

"It's best that you came straight here," Martin agreed. His voice granted absolution but his eyes made it clear that Martin would have gone after the intruders without a second thought.

"After all," Martin continued. "If you didn't evade them, we wouldn't know anything except what's been on the telly."

Martin directed his attention toward one of the ever-present videotape players that were scattered throughout the house like sentinels.

The director slapped in a tape on a wide-screen unit facing the bed. When he pressed the *Play* button, the screen came to life with the smoking ruins of the farmhouse.

It was a news broadcast "explaining" away the tragedy that had shattered the tranquillity in the south of England earlier that night.

"They're calling it a gangland war," Martin said. "First reports suggested an accident with some volatile chemicals kept on the farm. Then they put together a better story. The victims all had very disturbing records. Murderers of the worst stripe."

"These weren't police," Whitehouse said. "They were like nothing I've ever seen."

"Yes," Derek said. "They sound quite good. Someone deserving our very best." He turned up the volume of the videotape that was focusing on a trim newswoman winding down her story. *"Actually the cold-blooded killing between two rival mobs . . ."*

Martin laughed, then flicked off the videotape.

"Rivals, yes. Mobs, no," he said. "The truth is so malleable in the hands of professionals. No matter. Soon a couple of rumors will reach our good friend Crowell, and truth will out on INS. Our truth at least."

Adam Whitehouse felt relieved. But there was still one thing nagging at him. The merc captain might give away leads to Shock Troupe.

"No," Martin said, when Whitehouse mentioned it. "A couple of them survived but fortunately Kruge is dead. That came on the telly because Kruge was the centerpiece of their gangland slaying scenario. Besides, even if he survived, he didn't know me as Derek Martin."

Martin rewound the videotape. "Too bad you didn't have a camera with you tonight. You could have captured it all on film. That is, if you had lifted your head long enough to do so."

The director clapped his hands, his signal that the matter was over. "Now," he said, ushering White-house to the door. "There is someone else I must debrief."

12

Walker Jessup left the Mayfair town house early in the morning. He was feeling extremely secure.

Mayfair was one of the most watched-over areas in Britain. The intelligence services maintained surveillance over their allies, simultaneously protecting and keeping track of them. They also kept an eye out for ambassadors and attachés from hostile countries.

And it was all absorbed by machines of listening grace, Jessup thought. At least if he was hit it would be very well documented.

Discretely concealed cameras monitored the street from above. So did the well-armed guards who had become fixtures in Mayfair, ready to respond to any suspicious activity. For that reason, Jessup conducted his activity elsewhere.

After walking to a nearby café, a routine he established several mornings in a row, he continued on his way rather than return to Mayfair. He moved as swiftly as his bulk allowed, taking a succession of taxis at random before finally exiting at the London Docklands. The area was covered with scaffolding for new building projects going up all along the waterfront.

A car waited for him at the Surrey Docks. The driver, a British-born operative for the NSA, whisked him out to the countryside.

On the ride to the rendezvous, Jessup did his best to hide his near state of exhaustion, both from the driver *and* himself. Although he'd ridden more than walked, the fatigue still got to him.

His past life of extravagant dinners was wearing on him. He needed to sweat off the pounds just like the old days, and one of these days, he thought, he'd have to make a final decision to get back in shape.

It didn't help matters that his crew, or rather the crew that chose to use him as a power broker, were all in the best shapes of their lives. He had been becoming more self-conscious in their presence of his handicap of pounds. The SOBs were hard driven and hungry for life, and they were well equipped for it.

The Fixer was just plain hard driven and hungry.

BARRABAS PARKED the Range Rover on the side of the road. A light mist was falling, making the brush surrounding the lodge look green and lush.

He stepped up the wooden planks of the lodge and walked down a long, enclosed porch. What used to be a sizable picture window had been freshly boarded.

A sign with faded letters still partially visible hung over the entrance. *Tourist Information Center*. Jessup had chosen a suitable location for their meet.

Jessup swung open the inside door as Barrabas grabbed the screen door. Barrabas glanced up at the sign and said, "How appropriate."

Jessup laughed. "It always was a good cover. People could come and go all day long and no one would suspect."

The former tourist information center was one of several similarly abandoned places throughout the country. It had served as an authentic tourist center, safehouse and now a secure meeting place convenient to London.

Barrabas sat at a long table in a middle room that smelled of forest and old wood like a camp. Judging from the extra bulge beneath Jessup's jacket, it was an armed camp.

"You feeling any heat?" Barrabas asked.

"No more than usual," Jessup answered. "You're the one who felt the real heat. How did it go at New Forest?"

"It was a success two times over. First, we hit them before they even knew what was happening. Second, the little show we put on finally convinced Laird to give us full rein. It was more like a tryout. We didn't get cut, and now we get to know who the real players are."

Jessup nodded.

The two men went over the recent hit and the intel accumulated from the NSA and the Brits. They had been around long enough to realize what the New Forest hit had accomplished.

British intelligence had monitored the arrival of the mercs ever since they arrived, one by one, into the country. The Brits could have steered Barrabas to the new mercs at any time, but instead kept it hidden. After their surveillance people vacuumed all the intel they could get from the house, they turned over the mercs to the SOBs to see if they lived up to their covert reps.

They did, and then some.

Laird gave them his full backing. Now the hunt was on. Another door had opened for him, and the SAS liaison was furnishing Barrabas with as much intelligence as he could handle.

Barrabas wouldn't have committed his people to the strike just for a tryout. But when he learned from Laird that the Hamburg operators were going to hit Russian and American targets in an attempt to discredit the "lawless" operations of the intelligence services in the U.K., Barrabas decided it was time to go in.

It didn't hurt matters that the SOBs went into action right after the Shock Troupe assassination of one of Britain's top people.

"Now they know they're not the only sharks in the sea," Barrabas said. "There could be some shake-ups in their organization. As well, some of the survivors might have an interesting word or two about Shock Troupe."

Jessup indicated his agreement with that perspective, then proceeded to fill Barrabas in on their main contact with the NSA, Tsar Nicholas. Ever since he'd been announced as a target of Shock Troupe, the NSA man was chafing at the bit. "He wants the matter solved. Quick. And he's burning to come over here himself. The man is looking for miracles."

"Tell him I don't raise the dead," Barrabas scoffed. "As a matter of fact, we do just the opposite. Miracles don't fit into our contract." Then again, Barrabas thought, Billy Two might have a different opinion.

"I'll put Nicholas off as long as I can," Jessup said. "But as I said, he's tired of being under fire with no one to shoot at."

Barrabas studied the red-faced giant who sat across from him. It appeared he'd spent all the energy at his command and was getting agitated, thinking of another meal to restore him.

"What next?" Jessup asked.

Barrabas leaned back. He smoothed his hands along the table's worn surface. "While Laird is chasing down some more links to Shock Troupe, he's arranged a sit-down with one of his sources."

"Who's that?"

"Our most reliable enemy in the world," Barrabas remarked. "The KGB."

"So it's true then," Jessup said. "It looks like a KGB operation gone sour, and now they're burning their bridges."

"And they want to use us as the torches," Barrabas added. "But for now we'll play their game and see what we can stir up."

"Give them my regards," Jessup said.

Barrabas laughed, translating the scowl that accompanied Jessup's words as *"Give 'em hell!"*

KGB OFFICERS in London preferred to frequent the same restaurant for a variety of reasons, the least important being the quality of the food served. Partly it served the purpose of establishing their own turf so there would always be supporters around in the event of trouble.

There was yet another benefit. The informal hangouts were considered neutral territory where they could conduct "unofficial" business with their counterparts in the British and American agencies.

The restaurant the KGB currently used for many of their sit-downs was privately owned and operated. But a good number of the waiters and cooks happened to be members in good standing of MI5.

Nile Barrabas passed through a gauntlet of KGB associates whose ample bulk took up half a dozen tables in the Brompton Road restaurant chosen for the meet.

The man he came to see was waiting at a table in the back like a king in the midst of his court.

Barrabas eyed Vitaly Starkovich steadily as he drew closer, ignoring the muscle who glared at the chief SOB.

The KGB man at the table was serene-looking, but Barrabas knew a man didn't get this far in the KGB by tap-dancing his way through embassy parties. The man had enemies from the West to deal with as well as maintain his position in his intelligence service.

The Russian stood as Barrabas approached. Up close, Vitaly was a sleeker version of the men stationed around him. He was strong and fit but he was lean, and he wore a finely tailored suit. His thick hair had turned silver with swaths of brownish-rust on the sides.

"Welcome to my country," he said.

"A bit premature, isn't it?" Barrabas said. "Last I looked there was still a queen sitting on the throne."

"Of course. I meant my place of residence."

Barrabas smiled at the pun. The man was the chief of KGB operations, the *Rezident* of the London embassy.

"If you mean the House of Cards," Barrabas said, "I know it well."

It was common knowledge among the intelligence services who was who in the ranks of the opposition. Just in case Barrabas hadn't known that, the Soviet had deliberately pointed out that he was the *Rezident*, to either impress him or intimidate him. He expected to deal with someone of considerable weight.

Barrabas was immune to such rank-pulling, whether from his own side or from hostile services. Titles didn't matter, but what *did* matter was the *Rezident's* past work at the embassy, which unfortunately for the British was quite exceptional. As the head of Section 5, Starkovich's task was to plan for the theoretical destruction of Great Britain, part and parcel. With a vast network of legal and illegal agents, Starkovich had analyzed and targeted the Achilles heels of Britain's defense.

That kind of information was then acted upon by the KGB, or it was fed to terrorist or nationalist groups to wreak what havoc they could.

Barrabas was grateful that at least the Soviet operative was working in the open, which spared him the extra unpleasantness of dealing with a high-ranking KGB man who was posing as an underling.

The KGB had a fondness for having their chauffeurs actually be KGB officers who outranked the Soviets attached to the London embassy. The chauffeurs and clerks could wield awesome power, like Russian Clark Kents reverting to true form at nightfall.

But the man was a legitimate spook, not even a trade official, which typically was the all-purpose umbrella used by spook agencies the world over. Although in a way, the *Rezident* really did have something to trade this time around.

"So what are we talking about?" Barrabas said, after sitting at the table. "I'm always interested in making new friends, but you and I usually don't see eye to eye."

"We do now."

"Explain," Barrabas said.

"What's your hurry?"

Barrabas's response was curt. "People are dying. That's justification enough."

There was another reason for Barrabas to get to the matter directly, rather than in a roundabout manner. Like their counterparts in the CIA and MI5, KGB officers took every chance to recruit friends from other services. Barrabas intended to make it clear that he wasn't interested in wearing a yoke.

"A drink, then," the KGB officer suggested.

Barrabas nodded. "Whiskey," he said. "No ice. And make it American."

Vitaly smiled. "American it is."

After the waiter had been summoned and the order placed, Vitaly got down to business. "We are compiling a list of names in our files," Vitaly said. "British nationals and foreign mercenaries. Sometimes in the interest of peace we share this information."

Rather than spell things out with straight answers, Vitaly liked to play a guessing game so he could control the conversation. A life spent in the intelligence trade did that to a person.

"As in New Forest?" Barrabas said.

Vitaly gave him a confirming glance.

"So?" Barrabas said. "Now you've got another Christmas list of who's been naughty or nice?"

The officer tilted his head. "Naughty?"

"Like a hit list," Barrabas said. "Instead of coal for Christmas you'll give them lead."

The *Rezident* nodded, but it was clear he was losing track of the slang used by Barrabas. Although he'd mastered the language well, many nuances were still out of reach.

"The list is important," Vitaly insisted. "When I approached Brendan—excuse me, when I approached one of our British friends, he didn't want to be involved. Apparently you have a greater interest."

"I'm interested in Shock Troupe. If you know anyone connected to it, then yes, I'm ready to listen."

Vitaly Starkovich talked about the British entertainment business. He seemed to know most of the players, almost like a starry-eyed fan of the glamorous.

"Why are you telling me all this?" Barrabas asked, although he already knew the reason. At least two KGB officers had not returned to their embassy. One had a fatal hit-and-run accident. Another one was a suicide on the moors. Since the operatives were far afield from their legitimate turf, the Russian embassy hadn't made any inquiries.

In fact, when the Brits contacted the embassy to discuss the remains of the agents, the Soviets expressed surprise. These men were missing? How did they get so far from London? The Brits didn't press the issue. The men were dead. They let the Soviets claim the bodies.

The incident opened up channels with the KGB, channels that brought Barrabas to the Brompton Road restaurant.

"You can't get rid of people simply by putting their names on a list," Barrabas said. "This isn't Russia."

Vitaly shrugged. "You'll discover easily enough that many of these people are connected to the terrorists. Unfortunately we don't know the leader of the cell yet, but we may soon find out. With your help, maybe sooner."

"What do you want us to do?" Barrabas asked.

"What you do best," the KGB officer said.

Barrabas leaned back in the chair and drained the last of the American whiskey. "We're just negotiators."

"Then we ply the same trade," Vitaly answered knowingly.

"What can you give me?"

"As I told you. Follow up on these names and I'm sure you'll be able to find the truth."

"Or its distant cousin," Barrabas said.

The KGB agent looked amused. "Truth is relative, but in this case we haven't altered it one bit. Good luck." He raised his hand to summon the waiter. "Oh, by the way," he added, returning his attention to Barrabas, "do you follow the trades?" He lifted the folded newspaper he'd been reading, revealing a glossy magazine.

Barrabas looked at the gaudy cover of the magazine. It was called *SINEMATIC* and was subtitled *Forbidden Films*.

"I thought you folks only read the classics," Barrabas said.

"You will find some classic material in there."

Barrabas leafed through the magazine. Several photographs and photocopied material had been inserted throughout the magazine pages. The photos were old. Many of the subjects were in 60s costumes, men with Beatle boots and scraggly Vandykes, the women with thigh-high vinyl boots, miniskirts, and straight beatnik hair.

Barrabas rolled up the magazine. "Thanks. I was hoping for more, but it's a start."

"Perhaps at our next meeting we'll have more to exchange."

Barrabas studied the KGB officer. "Yes," he said, staring into his eyes. "Maybe by then I'll be able to prove who was behind these people from the start."

13

Out of a tunnel of darkness, he emerged into the confines of a small room. What was he, Thomas Crowell, to do amidst the hum and throb of electricity that pervaded the room?

Then he saw the pistol on a table and picked it up.

Slowly he turned toward a man on the other side of the table. It was Derek Martin. Without permitting himself a moment of doubt, the newsman leveled the gun at Derek Martin's face.

The director looked frightened, realizing for the first time that he'd tangled with the wrong man.

"That's right, you son of a bitch," Crowell said, and pulled the trigger.

The explosion filled the room, wrapping him in a cocoon of deafening sound as the bullet struck Martin in the forehead and ripped his temple open. Blood spurted like a fountain, and the director dropped to the floor. For a moment he looked like a headless chicken, totally covered with blood.

Then he collapsed.

Crowell sighed and put the gun back down on the table. He exhaled loudly and hung his head dejectedly.

"Not bad," Martin said, sitting up. He got to his feet and wiped some of the blood away, but the thick red fluid covered his upper body like a cape. "But you've got to put more anger into it." Martin handed the pistol to Crowell and said, "Try again."

Crowell screamed and fell back into the darkness.

It was the wrong dream again. Then, as if the dream was a film that had been rolled back, he was back in the room. The gun was on the table.

Crowell picked up the gun. He walked to the door and went down the hall to where his friend Roger was waiting, Roger the cameraman who'd also been taken prisoner along with himself.

Roger jumped from the table when Crowell stepped into the room. The door slammed behind him.

"Thank God, Tom!" Roger said. "I thought you were dead . . ." He threw his arms around Crowell.

They'd traveled all over Europe together, climbing through scrapes, helping each other come home alive from the battlefields they covered.

Now they had a chance again.

"We've got problems, Roger," Crowell said, breaking free from the embrace. His voice sounded flat, echoing around the walls of the enclosed room.

"Yeah, but we're together at least. Man, I've been so scared—"

"Take a look at the door," Crowell said.

Roger looked at the door, his eyes full of questions—questions that Crowell answered with a shot in the back of the skull, blowing his brains out.

Blood covered the floor, and it felt like sticky mud as he tried to slog his way through it. But the blood rose, and it was clinging to him like molasses, pulling him down. He was swimming in it now, its coppery taste filling his mouth, drowning in it.

"NOOOOOO!"

THOMAS CROWELL SPRANG straight up like a jack-in-the-box, suddenly wide-awake in his office at the INS tower. His legs slipped off his chair and thumped loudly on the floor. He'd been sitting with his feet up on top of the long console of monitors.

"Are you okay?" Cynthia Lane asked. She had burst through his door and waited there like a Florence Nightingale of the airwaves.

Still wrapped in sleep, Crowell nodded. He felt as if the room was swirling around him. "I'm fine," he said. "Don't worry about it."

She stepped closer. "Look, if there's something you want to talk about—"

He lifted his hand. "No. Everything's fine. Just some dreams giving me trouble." Those dreams were never too far from the surface.

How loud did he scream? he wondered. His room was soundproofed for just about everything—except perhaps his screams that were born in the cavern inside his soul.

Cynthia Lane, so beautiful, so crisp, even at this ungodly hour, put her soft manicured hand on his shoulder. Where was she when he was coming up through the ranks? he wondered. Why were all the sirens only at the top?

"Sure you're okay?"

"I'm fine," he said. "Nothing's wrong."

"Okay," she said. "Look, I've just about got the first segment done for the next show." She dropped a labeled videotape on his desk. "If you want to look at it in the morning..."

"I'll do that," he said. "Thanks."

Cynthia was practically living at the INS building. Most of the staff put in hellish hours as the biweekly show neared airtime. But only Crowell himself lived in hell.

"Thanks again," he said. "But I've got some work to do."

She nodded and hurried from the room.

Crowell stared at the master console.

News feeds glared at him from several screens at once. The sound was turned down so that only a loud hum could be heard in the room. He worked best in white noise. White noise helped to block things out.

Data streams flickered by on the bottom of each screen, giving location, date and source of the picture.

He'd been staying at the Black Tower on Fleet Street around-the-clock to put together the latest edition of *The Crowell Crusade*.

It was nearly three in the morning, and his efforts to keep alert had left a trail of tepid cups of coffee around the room. Stacks of videotapes covered the console, all tapes he had to scan for Derek Martin.

That was the worst part of it, he thought.

Maybe he'd be able to live with himself if he had a chance to rationalize the way he'd murdered his partner to save his own life. But Martin was always near, never letting him forget it. He was always demanding more footage. Never giving him time to think.

The director had leeched him of all his contacts. Crowell gave up the addresses of all the high-level people he knew in the government—some of whom were subsequently assassinated. Any skeletons in the closet that Crowell had known about, were now also known by Martin.

Crowell was no longer a newsman. He was a puppet.

He was a wealthy one, but all of those pleasures, the women who knew his name wherever he went, the cars that he'd always associated with celebrities, and the penthouse suites he'd grown accustomed to—none of that meant anything to the shell of the man who occupied the top-floor office in the Black Tower.

He'd gone from a Covent Garden flat to a palatial home in Belgravia. Actually that had been really accomplished by the man who used to be Thomas Crowell. The real Crowell was living a ghostly existence, now and then popping out for a moment in the sun. But most of the time he was just another bit actor in the Shock Troupe theater.

The choice of Crowell's news reports was virtually dictated to him by Derek Martin. Even some of the narration was provided by the director of Shock Troupe. "It's got to have the right slant, mate," Martin would say. "Don't worry about it. We're in this thing together."

And the disinformation went out over the airwaves as Crowell's work. His name and his soul were blackened by the endless stream of propaganda that he poured from the INS building.

Crowell shook his head to clear it, but it was no use. He was still exhausted. He hoisted his feet back up on the console, hoping there still might be a good dream left inside him.

Crowell used to work in the trenches. He used to find the news and bring it to the people. Now he was just a grave digger.

But still he had his dreams, dreams of killing Derek Martin and salvaging what little was left of the man who used to be a real crusader.

Of course there was a way he could vindicate himself. A way he could partially restore his name and bring one more scoop to the screen.

It would be his final report.

But to do that, his shame would have to outweigh his fear. And his courage would have to outweigh them both.

Thomas Crowell closed his eyes and went looking for the right dream.

14

The on-screen war escalated.

Shock Troupe videotapes appeared on the BBC, INS and several other European programs.

They were invariably followed by rebuttals from the government and from media critics. But there were always plenty of talking heads to take up the cause of the media guerrillas. The phenomenon was known as *Shock Troupe Chic*.

Forgotten intellectuals and fading celebrities alike rallied to the cause, getting their name in the limelight once again by paying lip service to Shock Troupe's code of conduct. Many of them were eager to resurrect their careers by encouraging the ''justice'' of Shock Troupe or simply to call attention to themselves by getting involved in such a controversial issue.

The British government could have easily censored the media to prevent security-related matters from being discussed, but knowing that the information would be leaked sooner or later, they decided to meet the problem head-on. More could be gained by *not* interfering. They could watch for leaks to the media and see where the pro-Shock Troupe pieces turned up most frequently. Besides, British Intelligence had their own assets in the media. Their reporters and commentators did their best to portray Shock Troupe as the killers they really were.

One of their top assets wasn't even a member of the media, although he was often a subject of their coverage. Whenever they needed a substantial quote, reporters turned to Lyndon Dagleish, a former war hero and wealthy patron of the arts who'd put together a massive fortune in the past two decades.

A spry man in his early seventies, Dagleish seemed to have the kind of energy that would carry him through for another twenty years or so. Dignified and still in perfect shape, he was respected by poor and wealthy alike.

If anything worth covering happened on the London scene, Dagleish was certain to be in the thick of it. A tastemaker and trendsetter, he was an old friend of British Intelligence, who frequently used one of his cultural foundations as covers for their activities.

By the same token, Dagleish could tap the old-boy network whenever he wanted publicity for one of his pet projects. A few key interviews or articles generated by intelligence assets started the ball rolling. Coverage of his latest cause would soon mushroom through the media.

Dagleish more than paid back the old-boy network with his endorsements of their positions and denouncements of Shock Troupe assassinations. He'd been a voice of reason ever since Shock Troupe made their first tape.

As the media war progressed, Dagleish looked to be a certain winner, rapidly erasing support for Shock Troupe.

THE XERXES GALLERY on the Thames had scored a major coup when it secured the Bog People exhibit that featured a group of performance artists who'd taken the latest trend to the ultimate extreme.

In New York and Paris, artists were posing as their own creations, spray painting themselves blue, green or gold, and hanging themselves on the wall as ornaments of the twentieth century.

On occasion they would talk to people visiting the gallery. Other times they would sit still for hours, coming alive only when someone touched them. Then they would scream, fall over, or start a conversation with the person who approached them.

It was a bright but probably short-lived gimmick.

Perhaps the best example of its kind was currently showing at the Xerxes Gallery.

The Bog People artists painted themselves in the gray hues of ancient corpses recently unearthed in British and Scottish peat bogs. Those corpses were perfectly preserved, right down to the parting of hair and the expression of death. A permanent death mask.

But the real part of the gimmick was that the imitators of the bog people were dressed in modern clothing, all of it also painted in metallic hues. They wore business suits, jeans and dresses, and were displayed in an exhibit that resembled the ancient bogs, complete with trees, sacrificial crosses and pagan icons spread all about.

The gallery had been packing in audiences and doing stellar business ever since the exhibit began. Word spread through newspapers and word-of-mouth, and soon anyone who was anyone trekked to the gallery just outside London.

So many people had to be turned away that the gallery began accepting reservations from the general public. To ensure that celebrities showed up in appropriate numbers, special invitations were sent out to the people who mattered in the art world—people like Lyndon Dagleish.

CAROLYN DRAKE LOOKED LIKE a million dollars, which was approximately what she'd cost her former husband, Lew Drake, for an amicable divorce. The settlement included the gallery she had "started from scratch," and she was determined to make a go of it.

Like the gallery itself, Carolyn was a work of art. Tall and statuesque with a bust of operatic proportions, she wore a subdued and mysterious smile that made her look as if she were about to devour someone. Her prey were exotic upper-class creatures who'd built nest eggs of millions of pounds.

At nine-thirty at night, she had flashed that smile for the personal benefit of Lyndon Dagleish, personally greeting him at the cathedral-shaped glass door entrance.

Her eyes danced over his slim and trim figure, thinking that he was a fine upstanding catch, and even better, that he might kick the bucket fairly quickly.

Staff photographers were on hand to compile photographs of celebrities attending the gallery functions. They would later show up in brochures, as if the celebrities themselves were the exhibits rather than the art works that brought them there.

Camera flashes lit up Carolyn's radiant face as she beamed alongside the faintly amused Dagleish who had become adept at performing for photographers.

Then Lyndon Dagleish stood in line like everyone else approaching the Bog People exhibit. Unlike the others, however, he was flanked by bodyguards, two well-groomed men who concealed parabellums in their pinstripes.

They inched soundlessly along the carpets of the Xerxes Gallery, which had a plush but sterile feel to them as if an army of mad sweepers were lurking in the distance to whisk them clean again the moment the intruders were out of sight.

A young couple stood behind Dagleish's entourage as it neared the immobile figures, which included businessmen with briefcases, a woman in a revealing one-piece swimsuit, and a bare-chested construction worker leaning on a long steel mallet.

"Give your eyes a break, love," the woman said to her escort, who'd been ogling the silvery painted woman.

The walkway cut right through the bog set, so that the audience could talk, cajole or try to stare down the actors who were posing as statues.

Though they were cold to look at, they were warm to the touch. The "statues" were more outgoing than usual, shaking hands and carrying on conversations with the gallery patrons.

The bog woman seemed to get the most attention, although the entire exhibit was startling.

She glanced up at Dagleish as he neared.

"Been here long?" Dagleish asked.

"For ages," she said, smiling. It wouldn't matter what she said. Covered as she was with metallic gray paint, she looked like a statue come to life. Just to hear her speak produced an eerie sensation.

The bodyguards who had flanked Dagleish all along relaxed and took interest in the woman, too. They felt insulated enough. The people in line around them were harmless. The woman in the exhibit was fetching. Hovering around them was Carolyn Drake in the full magnificence of her icy beauty. Altogether, the visit was one of few perks for the security men.

They enjoyed it for all of one minute.

That's when the voluptuous "statue" reached out and slid her hand coyly up Dagleish's tie as if she wanted to straighten it out.

Dagleish was never one to turn down a fawning woman. He lowered his head slightly to make her task easier.

That's when she yanked hard on the tie, pulling him over to a bowing position.

The bog man with the hammer swung it with force and brought it down on the back of Dagleish's head. Though it didn't behead him, the act had the look of an ancient execution.

The sickening crunch of metal on bone was followed by the sound of Dagleish falling to the floor, his elegantly dressed body sprawling among the tufts of grass and silvery pools of water.

The security men had been taken totally by surprise. Was it all part of the act? they'd wondered when the girl grabbed Dagleish. That question stayed on their minds for a few fatal moments.

As the hammer came down on Dagleish, different sorts of hammers came down on the two bodyguards.

Before they could react to the slaughter of the man in their charge, two bog men in business suits leveled submachine guns at them. It had only taken them a second to grab the SMGs from their briefcase props.

The bodyguard closest to Dagleish had leaped forward, instinctively heading toward the armed men in an attempt to close the gap. Retreating would have made him an easier target. Besides, there were too many innocents standing behind him. His hand was snaking inside his jacket for his holstered weapon when the assassins opened up on him with selective fire.

The first bodyguard was stitched from the neck downward. Gaping wounds blossomed dark red as his head tilted awkwardly and his body seemed to fold in upon itself.

The second bodyguard, a smaller and stouter man, had moved quickly. He backed up a couple of steps and actually removed his automatic from his holster.

A three-round burst kicked him off his feet.

The line of patrons collapsed as if they too had been shot down. But most of them were diving for cover or had simply been knocked off their feet as sudden panic swept through the room.

Though the exhibit had been fake, the weapons were real. So was the blood rapidly spreading in red halos around the slain bodyguards.

Then the screaming began as the well-dressed patrons scrambled and clawed for the exits in total panic.

One of the attackers flicked the selector to full-auto and sprayed the gallery. Bullets chomped into paintings on the wall. Picture frames splintered and cracked as they landed, spilling the wounded canvas portraits onto the floor. Statues broke, arms and heads flying, as the business-suited bog men strafed the decorous interior of the gallery.

They laid down a steady fusillade to keep back any would-be heroes or other armed bodyguards in the crowd. Glass display cases exploded into tinkling shards, and the killers made their way out through the back of the gallery—their latest performance piece never to be forgotten.

Several vehicles waited at the back. Vans, pickup trucks and passenger cars moved out in a phalanx of screeching tires that signaled the grand finale of the Bog People exhibit.

Only three of the patrons remained inside, their lifeless bodies still as statues.

Within an hour of the attack, news stations around London received a blizzard of calls.

Shock Troupe took credit for the mission. They also gave their reasons why, providing a brief but accurate dossier of Lyndon Dagleish's career.

True, he had served as a commando in operations at the end of World War II. And admittedly he had stayed in the service to assist settling the upheaval in Germany in the aftermath of the war. But in the wake of his heroism, opportunism arose.

Assigned to Art Squad Recovery, the British unit responsible for recovering art plundered by the Nazis, Dagleish rose to prominence in officially divided Germany. He also involved himself in the unofficial division of spoils.

Some charges were leveled against him: missing works of art that had last passed through his hands; murders of black market gang members were traced to his operation.

Theft and murder—although practiced wholesale in the war—weren't so welcome in the chaos that fell upon Germany for several years. But they weren't noticed that much either.

Dagleish left the service a rich man. Along with his huge black market profits, he had several caches of art works to start his career as a collector. To get that fortune, Dagleish had left several bodies buried in unmarked graves throughout Germany, most of them criminals.

After a year of lying low in London, Dagleish began his rapid rise to the top, and soon was known as a wealthy philanthropist who backed all the right causes.

He totally succeeded in burying his past, until Shock Troupe caught up with him.

15

Barrabas propped his boot-shod feet on the wooden table. A few drops of amber liquid sloshed onto the table from a half-full tumbler of whiskey. He folded his arms across his chest, and as Walker Jessup entered and sat at the other side of the table, subjected him to a long glare.

Barrabas was the one to call for the rendezvous at the Tourist Information Center.

The lodge wasn't as musty, with the warm spring sun beating through the windows.

"What've you got?" Jessup said.

"I've got our man," Barrabas said.

Jessup looked up so swiftly that his double chin wobbled, victim of a gluttonous jet lag trying to catch up to the rest of his body.

"Who is it?" Jessup asked.

"We think it's a movie director," Barrabas said.

"Does he possess a *name*?"

"He's got several," Barrabas answered. "He used at least half a dozen names to put out scores of movies ever since the sixties."

"Do you know his real one?"

"Derek Martin," Barrabas said.

Jessup frowned. "Did this information come from our KGB friend?"

Barrabas laughed shortly. "No," he said. "It's one that he *didn't* give me. That's how we know it's good."

Barrabas explained his reasoning. Vitaly Starkovich sponsored Shock Troupe in the beginning, but now was burning both ends of the candle—with the SOBs in the middle. The KGB *Rezident* gave enough hints to the SOBs so they would make things hot for Shock Troupe. But he didn't identify the leader, hoping Shock Troupe would step back in line again.

"If he didn't give the name to you, where did you get it?"

Barrabas tapped his finger on the splintery table. "Our good friend Vitaly left out a name that should have been on the list. Derek Martin's name was conspicuous by its absence."

"That's not very conclusive."

"We've got other sources," Barrabas said, and updated Jessup on the activities of the others SOBs who had been unleashed on the exploitation movie community.

Nanos and O'Toole had tracked the slain actress to Shock Troupe, using several early movies she made for a number of pseudonymous directors. With dossiers compiled by British intelligence, they and the rest of the SOBs put the moves on several distributors.

Since many of the exploitation distributors overlooked small items like paying taxes to the government, they were in a mood to cooperate. Especially when they learned they could pick up some easy money. After fattening the distributors' wallets, the

SOBs managed to uncover a strong connection between Gabriella Fucshin and Derek Martin.

"That's good," Jessup said. "But is it good enough?"

Barrabas nodded. "I think we'll know soon enough. Vitaly has contacted me through Laird. He wants to set a meet—giving me a chance to eliminate the director of Shock Troupe."

"Do you believe him?" Jessup asked.

"Of course not," Barrabas said. "But I do believe Derek Martin will be there. The way I see it, Vitaly can't lose. If I'm quicker on the draw, then he's a hero. If Shock Troupe beats me to it, then Vitaly is back in their good graces. They'll be a team again."

Jessup nodded. "That sounds par for the course. But if you go to that meet, most likely you'll be taken out."

"That's right," Barrabas said.

"You going to meet them?"

"Yeah," Barrabas said. He paused. "But not the way they think."

Jessup had been sitting back all along, wondering what was wanted of him. They were not engaged in social chat, and Barrabas, who was looking even more stern than usual, had spelled things out in great detail. That could only mean he was leading Jessup down the path. He wanted something from the Fixer, something the Fixer didn't want to give.

Barrabas was silent as he toyed with the whiskey tumbler, using his foot on the table as an anchor while he tilted his chair back and forth.

"What do you want me to do?" Jessup finally asked.

"Bring me the head of NSA's covert ops."

Jessup stared at him. "Are you crazy? You told me you'd abort the mission if Teddy Nicholas forced his way in! Now you want him in..."

"Shock Troupe made it clear they wanted Teddy Nicholas dead. They even put him on their damned *Coming Attractions* list. So if the NSA Tsar wants to be used as bait, then he can be my guest. I'll put him on the hook myself."

Jessup's face reddened. "If this goes wrong, we'll all be out of jobs—"

"If this goes wrong," Barrabas said, "I'll be dead and you won't have a crew anymore. Let's just do it."

Jessup nodded. "Okay. I'll give Nicholas the green light. And we'll see what happens. Now, are you sure Derek Martin's the one?"

"I'm sure enough," Barrabas said, swirling the half-full whiskey tumbler in his hand. "But if we do this the slow way, move in on him now and conduct surveillance and all that jazz, we might find nothing. He'll play innocent and just lie low for a while. We get nothing. If we do it my way and they take the bait— then they'll lie low forever." Barrabas smiled and placed the tumbler back on the table.

Jessup looked at the tumbler. Hating to see anything go to waste, he asked, "Aren't you going to drink that?"

"This?" Barrabas said. "No, it was just a victory drink for finding out who our man was. I already had my share."

"So finish it," Jessup said.

"Can't drink it all yet," Barrabas said. "So far it's only half a victory." He stood up. "When it's a full victory, I'll come back for the other half."

"And if it isn't?"

Barrabas slid the tumbler across the table. "My treat," he said.

16

Mahogany Row was the name given to the ninth-floor offices of the National Security Agency's headquarters at Fort Meade, Maryland, where NSA officers ran the world's most effective intelligence empire.

Tsar Nicholas was the name given to the man who spearheaded many of their operations. Second in power only to DIRNSA, the director of the NSA, Teddy Nicholas was a Russian expert and the staunchest supporter of joint U.S. and British intelligence gathering operations.

That made him a key target for Shock Troupe.

It also made him fighting mad. Normally an approachable yet determined spy chief, the Navy veteran was chafing from the discomfort of the excessive precautions his people were taking. Yet he knew they were not doing it to amuse themselves or to alleviate their boredom.

Electrified fences, armed guards and state-of-the-art monitoring systems secured NSA's "secret city" at Fort Meade from the world at large. When he was in his office, Tsar Nicholas was perhaps one of the safest individuals in the Western world.

His people were determined to extend that security outside his office as well. Twenty-four hours a day their best operatives insured his safety.

The coverage would continue as long as Shock Troupe had him in their sights. It had begun the moment Shock Troupe released film of the Tsar in their *Coming Attractions*.

He was shadowed wherever he went, from NSA headquarters to his rural retreat in Maryland. The shadows were a rotating army of security guards who planned every movement ahead of time so the proper escort could be in place. The way things were going, he expected them to post a guard under his bed before he and his wife could sleep in it.

Already the house was filled with "guests," including a perfect couple—a blond cheerleader type and a square-jawed quarterback—who happened to be NSA agents. "Barbie and Ken," he called them.

Tsar Nicholas was a prisoner and he wanted out. He was ready to put an end to it, even if that meant putting himself at risk.

The first time he'd broached the idea with the Fixer, Walker Jessup wouldn't even listen to it. After an SOB operation was given the go-ahead, Barrabas insisted on calling the shots. The Tsar respected that. His rise through the intelligence community had been accelerated by his willingness to delegate responsibility and let people do what they were best at—and do it their own way.

But after all, Tsar Nicholas was the man who bankrolled the operation. He was the top man in the covert hierarchy, and one whose privileges included the ability to pull rank.

At ten in the morning, braced with a cup of strong coffee after a sleepless night, Tsar Nicholas was at his desk planning how he would take personal control of the SOBs operation when he received a call from Walker Jessup in London on a secure line.

Usually their calls began with a moment or two of chatting. After all, they'd been friends for a while. But as soon as the NSA chief recognized Jessup's voice, he snapped, "Dammit, Jessup, I'm coming over."

"You're the boss," Jessup said.

Just to make sure the Fixer understood what he was talking about, the Tsar said, "And I plan on taking care of that problem we discussed earlier."

"Yes, sir," Jessup said.

"Good. And make arrangements for me to meet your man the moment I get there."

"Of course," Jessup said.

There wasn't a trace of the usual combativeness in the Fixer's voice. He too could be stubborn—one of the reasons he enjoyed using Jessup. But something was up. Why the change of heart? "Okay," Nicholas said. "That's settled. Now why did you call?"

"Call?" Jessup said.

"Yes. You called me. What was it about?"

"Oh, nothing, sir. It'll keep until you get here."

It wasn't that many hours later that they met face-to-face. On the transatlantic flight Nicholas had time to ponder his recent conversation with Jessup. But even after they met at Heathrow, the answers had to wait.

A discreet parade of armored cars then made their way to a safehouse in the country where, Jessup informed him, Barrabas was waiting.

"Good of you to see me," Nicholas said, shaking hands with Nile Barrabas in a glass-walled room with a well-equipped bar.

"We're on the same team," Barrabas replied, shrugging off the sarcasm of one of the most powerful men to use his team's services.

"At least we agree on something," Nicholas said.

Both men sat in a couple of easy chairs flanking a marble-topped coffee table. They got right down to business.

Nicholas leaned forward confidingly in his chair. With his neatly trimmed beard, and the airs of a college professor, he gave the impression that what he had to say had been carefully rehearsed. "Let me explain what I have in mind..."

Tsar Nicholas was far removed from the trenches and the trench coats. But not all that much time had passed since he'd been in combat, and he still felt capable of serving in the front lines.

He exploded in anger when Barrabas deep-sixed the idea of using a heavily-armed Nicholas to lure Shock Troupe guns in close to him.

"We'll do it my way," Nicholas said.

"Not a chance," said the stone-faced mercenary with the shock of white hair.

Nicholas glared at him, but Barrabas disregarded his anger. "Sir, no disrespect, but I don't think you're up to this. It really has been too long since you've been in the field."

"I can handle myself."

Barrabas laughed.

Suddenly Tsar Nicholas leaned forward and sprung. The punch had been building up steam for months now. Though its immediate destination was Barrabas's face, the real target was the faceless terrorist who'd made the threat on his life.

The punch streaked toward Barrabas, then stopped in midair. The fist made a loud whack as it connected with Barrabas's raised palm and was enclosed by it.

For a minute they were locked in that tableau, then the NSA man shrugged and was released right away.

"Sorry," Nicholas said. "I don't know why I did that."

"Being under the gun months on end takes its toll," Barrabas said. "No explanation necessary." The level look in Barrabas's eyes was an admission that he'd goaded the Tsar into taking that punch only to prove his point. "However if that's the best you can do, sir, you won't have a chance. Your role in this decoy action *has* to be strictly window dressing. You stay out of the line of fire."

Nicholas said, "You have the nerve to talk like that to me? Do you know what I could do to you?"

"Right now, not much," Barrabas said. "But I do know what you've been doing for our country. In fact, sir, I've put my life on the line a number of times to help you do just that, and so have my people. And we're not going to throw away everything we've gained just because you want to come in like a cowboy with your six-shooters blazing."

Nicholas folded his arms, looking once again like a cool-headed professor. "Right," he said. "*You're* the guys who come in with the six-shooters."

"Six-shooters or laser-locked SMGs," Barrabas said. "Whatever it takes."

"We'll do it your way," he said.

"Good," Barrabas said. "Here's the game plan. You've traveling with a small army of plainclothesmen. Anyone with proper training will notice that. It's like waving a flag to Shock Troupe saying, *'Here I am, come and get me.'* And they'll try to do just that—as soon as we leak the best spot for them to kill you."

Barrabas explained the plan. Nicholas would appear on television, praising the close ties between the U.S. and Britain. He'd also take a swipe at Shock Troupe, labeling them as petty thieves and murderers who couldn't keep him out of a free country.

The media coverage would climax with his announcement of a brief stop at an abandoned government site the U.S. was leasing from Britain to build a communications station. Although a veil of secrecy would shroud the site, a number of leaks would pinpoint it for Shock Troupe—a former World War II proving grounds.

The visit would be announced well ahead of time so Shock Troupe could plan their move against him.

"What if they don't take the bait?"

"I can't imagine them not going for it," Barrabas said. "Shock Troupe wants the U.S. out of Britain. You're the next best thing to Uncle Sam itself. If they knock you out, it'll be a symbolic victory for them. After their usual smear treatment, they'll claim you were grandstanding and brought it on yourself."

Tsar Nicholas nodded. "Bring it on," he said.

VITALY STARKOVICH passed the photograph to Derek Martin in the back seat of a black limo that had been rented by one of the KGB's agents in place.

It was touring the East Anglia coastline, which appeared gloomier than usual through tinted windows that were now streaked with rain.

Although they recently had been opponents, both men felt safe in the other's presence.

Under the terms of etiquette worked out by Martin for the rendezvous, Whitehouse was sitting in the front seat with the KGB driver. Both he and the driver sat silently, each of them holding an unholstered automatic pistol. A bullet-resistant soundproofed window separated them from the parley taking place in the back.

The director of Shock Troupe looked at the photograph of the mercenary that had been taken in a KGB-frequented restaurant.

The man's face was weathered. His hair was streaked with white. But he didn't look old. He looked like a survivor.

"What's this about?" Martin asked. "This man wants a screen test?"

"That is the man looking for you," Vitaly said. "He might find you. *He's* the one who found your German friends. It seems that well-informed people have been giving him tips."

Martin nodded and looked at the KGB *Rezident.* "Who could that be, I wonder?"

They had worked together in the past, and though they had had a minor skirmish that had resulted in a couple of casualties on both sides, there was no reason they couldn't work together again.

"I told you our connections are severed permanently," Martin said. "I want to go my own way. Why do you persist?"

"This is a peace offering," Vitaly said. "It may help you. Then, someday, you may help me. Perhaps to start, you might refrain from exposing some of my people to the British."

The limo swooped soundlessly around a series of S-curves that followed the shore. A marshy tract of land ate away at the sides of the road, giving the passengers the sensation that at times they were riding on a bridge.

Martin leaned back into the soft cushion and draped his arm over the back seat. He glanced once more at the photo, then handed it back to Vitaly.

"You've been in contact with this man?"

"Yes."

"Where can I find him?" Martin asked.

"I believe he will find you."

Martin sighed. "What do you propose?"

"I can arrange a meeting," Vitaly said. "Where you can get the drop on him."

"And if I don't go?"

"Then this man may receive more tips about the man running Shock Troupe."

Martin nodded. "Things have been getting hot lately," he admitted. "All right, I believe we have a deal. One thing, though."

"Yes?" the Russian said.

"Is this the same deal you're giving him?"

Vitaly laughed. "As a matter of fact, it is. In a manner of speaking. I told him I had another lead to your group. He'll come to a sit-down with me. Naturally I won't show. And you can do whatever it is you have to do."

"Lead him to me, then," Martin said.

Vitaly nodded. He pressed a button on the armrest and spoke to the driver. "Bring our friends back to their cars," he said. "We are going home."

Martin noted the deliberateness of Vitaly's speech. Obviously the KGB man had arranged a couple of different codes for his driver. What would Vitaly have told him if Martin hadn't agreed? he wondered. Would they have tried to take out both Martin and Whitehouse?

He shrugged it off, thinking that in a way it would have been interesting. The matter would have been solved once and for all.

Of one thing he was certain. Derek Martin had come to the meeting fully prepared to act out whatever role was required. If it had been a trap, no one would have left the car alive.

17

The lighting that illuminated Thomas Crowell's office was suitable for broadcast quality.

Usually he kept the lights dim, but for the night's forthcoming occasion they were turned up almost all the way.

An expensive but very slim and light video camera was mounted on a tripod facing his desk. He checked himself in the monitor to see how he would appear on tape.

A faint halo effect surrounded his upper body.

Crowell laughed. He pushed off from the desk, his four-castered chair sliding smoothly across the thin carpeted office. He reached up and flicked the rest of the lights on to dispel the saintly illusion.

Back at his desk, he faced the video camera just as he'd done countless times before. Except he hadn't planned on having a cameraman behind it. Crowell ran the video camera with a remote control switch.

He looked into the lens as if he were looking right at a friend, a trick that most broadcasters used in order to establish their one-on-one sincerity with the viewer.

This time it wasn't a trick, he thought. It was time for Thomas Crowell to speak his own mind, and not the words put into it by Derek Martin.

He was calmer than he thought he would be. Part of that was his old professionalism returning, and the rest was born of the absence of fear.

He'd already faced the worst part. The men from British intelligence had swept through the INS building. None of them identified just what agency they worked for. But the presence of uniformed police bowing to their every wish proved that they wielded sufficient power.

The intelligence men checked everyone. News reporters. Broadcasters. Assignment editors. Celebrities as well as technical crew had been interrogated very politely and very thoroughly.

The interrogators seemed particularly interested in Crowell's escape from terrorists so long ago. How did he overcome one of them? How did he escape their subsequent pursuit?

"Hostages don't escape from terrorists," the man from intelligence said. "Unless the terrorists want them to."

Crowell shrugged it off. He was always quick with an answer. Excuses, lies and sometimes truth were his stock in trade. He could slant a story or tell the truth with equal sincerity.

They'd commented on the extensive coverage that INS had given to the Bog People exhibit, which coincidentally fanned public interest in the gallery.

And then they mentioned how efficient INS was after Dagleish was assassinated, having cameramen on the scene in record time—almost as if somebody had a crew on standby waiting for a late-breaking story.

The intelligence men seemed to be playing a cat-and-mouse game with Crowell. They treated everybody in the building in a likewise manner, but Crowell felt that he was the most hunted. Then the spooks left abruptly, moving their rolling inquisition to other sinners.

They would get him sooner or later. That much he knew.

Thomas Crowell had stayed alone in his office, swinging on a pendulum of guilt and fear. He didn't leave the office for days, but there was nothing unusual about that, not when he was working on a piece for broadcast. By the time the weekend arrived, he had assembled the material he needed for his latest broadcast. It was time to strike back.

He couldn't kill Derek Martin with a gun. He didn't have the temperament or the nerve for that. But he could kill him with the only skill he had.

Crowell glanced in the monitor one more time. His hair was combed neatly, his eyes were clear.

And, for the first time in ages, so was his conscience.

He pressed the *Record* button on the remote control unit, activating three videotape recorders at once. Then he welcomed the camera in his usual manner.

"Good evening, this is Thomas Crowell. Many of you know me as an investigative reporter. Some of you even think of me as a crusader. Tonight I would like to show another side of me."

It came easily. Unrehearsed and right to the point.

He explained how he'd been a good reporter once. How he was a good man. And he still would have been a decent sort if it hadn't been for Derek Martin.

He explained how he'd sent reporters not so much to cover stories but to compile dossiers and track movements of potential Shock Troupe targets. He explained how Shock Troupe worked, how they framed people and forced them into positions from which they couldn't escape.

"I didn't escape from my captors as I've previously claimed," Crowell said to the camera. "In fact, I was forced to execute one of my closest friends in order to go on living myself. But it hasn't been living at all. It has been dying. It has been hell."

He recounted the real story of the night he and his crew were captured by Shock Troupe terrorists and how that night had cast shadows over the rest of his life.

He spoke about a woman named Gabriella who came to him for help—and how he sent her to her death—a death that was shown in lurid color on the first Shock Troupe tape.

He revealed all he knew about Derek Martin, and went on to list the other accomplices of Shock Troupe.

And then he signed off for the last time, saying, "Good night. This has been Thomas Crowell."

He stopped the camera, rewound two of the videotapes and inserted them into small brown videotape mailers. He left his office, took the elevator down to the darkened mail room and then scattered the tapes among the outgoing INS mail.

When he returned to his office he sat behind his desk once again to deliver a postscript to his broadcast tape. He turned on the camera just as he turned the .38 revolver on himself and pulled the trigger.

The show was over forever. The blast knocked him off is chair, onto the floor and into a new dream.

BARRABAS PRESSED DOWN the lever on the phone in the Mayfair flat, cutting off his conversation with Vitaly Starkovich. The disconnect mechanism made a sound like a gun being cocked.

How appropriate, Barrabas thought as he cradled the receiver. In a way he'd just handed a loaded gun to the KGB officer. A gun in turn that would be handed over to the leader of Shock Troupe.

"Well?" Walker Jessup asked. He'd been leaning over a conference table to study an ordnance map of an English moor.

"Our friend Vitaly is upset at me canceling the rendezvous," Barrabas said. "In fact, I don't know if I can call him *my* friend anymore."

"You'll get over it," Jessup said.

Barrabas nodded, then summarized Vitaly's side of the phone call.

The KGB *Rezident* had been furious, although he'd done his best to keep his voice level on the phone. Vitaly had spent a lot of time setting up the meet where Barrabas could supposedly get the jump on the terrorist leader. Though Vitaly hadn't identified the director of Shock Troupe by name, Barrabas had no doubt that Derek Martin would have been at the rendezvous.

Barrabas was sufficiently vague about his reason for breaking the prearranged appointment with Starkovich. Vague enough to whet the man's curiosity. But it obviously had to be something important, something that Barrabas had no control over that made him cancel.

The date for the meeting coincided with Teddy Nicholas's scheduled appearance.

Since Barrabas had hinted on a security matter involving a superior, the KGB officer would soon put it together that Barrabas was attached to the security unit for the NSA man, Shock Troupe's long-running target.

Shock Troupe could take them both out at the same time. It was a perfect opportunity for both sides. The KGB man could disengage himself from the entire episode and let the director of Shock Troupe do what he must. The KGB would come through it unscathed.

At least, that was how it would appear on the surface. Behind the scenes, Barrabas already had his sappers undermining the illusion he'd fed to Vitaly Starkovich.

Barrabas made two more calls, the first to an isolated house on the Western coast of England near the Bristol Channel. The call put the SOBs on alert. He then called Lee Hatton who was surveilling the King's Glen estate to watch for any sign of activity on Derek Martin.

At that point, it was time for Barrabas to turn his attention to the map that Jessup was tracing with his hand, his pudgy finger slashing through the painted wilderness. "This is the way the NSA caravan will come," Jessup said. "The advance vehicles will stop here. The Tsar and a few British bigwigs will then make a tour of the site..."

Barrabas listened to the preparations that Jessup had worked out with the NSA chieftain.

The site for which the NSA was negotiating a lease faced the Bristol Channel and ran parallel to Exmoor, wild and secluded country ideal for NSA purposes—not that the NSA was actually going to set up shop there.

Barrabas heard Jessup outline the expected route of Tsar Nicholas and company.

Then the SOB commander stabbed his finger on a section of map showing a hilly, wooded rise. "And there's where Shock Troupe will probably make their kill."

"Yes, they will," Jessup agreed. "If you fuck up."

Barrabas straightened up and looked down at the map, scanning the abandoned shooting range and proving grounds once again.

18

Right after Alex Nanos hung up the phone, he said, "Barrabas wants us to move out." He looked over at Billy Two. The Osage was sitting on the floor, leaning back against the wall with his eyes closed. "Hey, Billy," Nanos said, "all astral flights are canceled. Stop thinking deep thoughts. We got work to do."

Billy Two stayed immobile.

Nanos approached him slowly and tapped his out-stretched foot. "Any questions, swami?"

Billy Two fired a glance at Nanos. Although he'd been catching sleep to prepare the way for a long trek in the wilderness, he wasn't about to enlighten Nanos. Let the man think he was lost in space. Billy Two pushed himself up on his feet and stretched, his long arms brushing against the ceiling. "Yeah, I got a question," he said.

"What's that?" Nanos asked.

"How many angels can dance on the head of a pin?"

Nanos cocked his head as if he were mulling it over. Then he said, "Would that be flamenco, waltz or polka?"

Billy Two shook his head, realizing that Nanos would spend an eternity avoiding the eternal question.

They headed down to the dining room where Hayes and O'Toole had an assortment of clips and weapons, mostly Heckler & Koch submachine guns and Browning Hi-Power pistols spread out on the table. The room smelled of metal and oil.

"Let's get packed, troops," Nanos said. "Barrabas wants us to move out."

"Just when this place was starting to feel like home," Billy Two said.

The others laughed. Though the house they were staying at had a good view of the sea, it was just a functional shell, nothing more. It was a typical safe-house, nothing out of the ordinary to attract interest. Just a place to assemble, pick up weapons—and wait.

But that was over now.

Within a matter of minutes they had their gear packed into the Range Rovers parked outside.

The four SOBs had been in readiness here ever since Barrabas had decided to bring Tsar Nicholas into the operation. They'd used the time to familiarize themselves with the area, visiting the abandoned shooting range and driving around the nearby access roads.

The time had come to put that knowledge to use.

THE SHALLOW STREAM cut a swath through moss-covered banks. Trees on both sides of the stream leaned on their neighbors, their branches struggling to dominate in the fight for sunlight. The banks themselves rose sharply and curved toward one another, as if they were conspiring to conceal the stream itself.

The shade and the steep-banked riverbed concealed Liam O'Toole and Alex Nanos as they slogged through the knee-high water.

Even if someone was watching, their forest green camos blended in perfectly with the surroundings. Their faces were ribboned with swatches of green and black. By keeping close to the steep banks, they were almost impossible to spot.

They moved quietly, the flowing of the water covering any sound of their movement as they patrolled the stream. It wound through the moor like a moat, encircling the proving grounds.

Billy Two and Claude Hayes moved across the moor, zigzagging through the woods.

The four-man team of SOBs had infiltrated the forest, feeling more at home each hour, each night. They cut through the wilderness like an unseen wolf pack staking out their territory.

But rather than wolves, they looked more like werewolves. They changed their silhouettes according to the terrain. Instead of presenting normal manlike outlines, they resembled creatures of the woods in their brush and leaf camouflage and matted animal-hair vest. They stalked the ground, determining the best place for someone to set an ambush.

Barrabas arrived on the third day of their watch, after making arrangements for the firefight—if it came off. So far there hadn't been any sign of Shock Troupe.

In the back of each SOB's mind was the nagging idea that they had chosen the wrong place. Shock Troupe wouldn't take the bait. Instead, while the

SOBs were occupied here, they would strike somewhere else.

The doubts grew strongest at night when every shadow was a potential enemy and every unquiet dream possibly their last.

But then Lee Hatton arrived.

There had been a lot of activity at Derek Martin's estate in King's Glen. Cars left the manor in ones and twos. Shock Troupe was on the move.

STEADY WHISPERS PASSED through the underbrush as the hissing of the wind skittered through the woods, gaining in volume like secrets passed from mouth to mouth. Long boughs shook and waved overhead, fanning moonlight over the moor.

Derek Martin stepped softly over the rolling proving grounds. They'd come the back way, scrambling through the wilds rather than announcing themselves by driving straight up to the splintered gates.

Wind pushed at his back, hurrying him along to the site he'd chosen for the ambush.

A long gully ran in a semicircle overlooking the most intact parcel of the training grounds, where a dirt road circled in front of the dilapidated entrance to the site. The road was overgrown with weeds and studded with gaping potholes. It looked impassable, but it would be an ideal spot for the *before-and-after* pictures so beloved by the authorities whenever they started out on such a huge reclamation project as this.

The road split off from the better-kept country road that sliced through the region in serpentine fashion.

Decades ago the abandoned site was a choice spot for sightseers who toured the wide expanse of wood, river and moor. But that had decreased as the wilderness reclaimed its own, collapsing the buildings and filling the trenches with high grass.

Few souls braved the area anymore. Shock Troupe reconnaissance units had driven by during the daylight hours, now and then pulling over to the side of the road. But no one traveled through the area at night. There was a haunted feel to the moors, almost as if the ghosts of the soldiers who trained here during World War II were lingering about, watching over the area of their birth as warriors.

But Derek Martin was in the business of making ghosts, not fearing them. Besides, they had come well in advance of the date for the arrival of Tsar Nicholas and the British collaborators selling him the land. No one would be there but men like Derek Martin and his detachment of Shock Troupers.

He had ten men with him and one woman. For Shock Troupe that was nearly a battalion. Though they were small, they could do more damage than a conventional army.

He spread his men out, familiarizing them with the strike zone, and just as important, the escape route.

They carried rifles, explosives and the most potent weapon of all, cameras to film their assault on the ultimate symbol of U.S. subversion of Britain.

Teddy Nicholas was going to be the very next star of Shock Troupe. Martin had no doubt this videotape would shoot to the top like a bullet.

ADAM WHITEHOUSE JOGGED down through the wooded incline, seeing how close he could come to the level ground where the NSA caravan would show. If he had to, he could rip off a clip on full-auto, then use the cover of the gully to make it back to the safety of the woods.

Even if it was a close pursuit, Whitehouse had the edge. Whatever kind of security men the NSA had, he doubted many of them could run through the woods at the breakneck speeds he was capable of. He'd spent his life as a stuntman. This stunt was just one more gig, and besides, he would be familiar with the terrain.

He might not even have to run. If things went according to Martin's plan, there would be no one left to give chase.

They'd already stashed some heavy equipment in the woods, along with caches of Sterling submachine guns they'd planted in the woods. Enough to wipe out a visiting band of dignitaries.

Whitehouse climbed back up the way he'd come. When he reached the top of the hill, he scanned the surroundings.

Something seemed a bit off. In some imperceptible way the woods didn't seem to catch the image that had been embedded in his brain.

Maybe it was just the clouds, he thought. They must have passed overhead, dropping a few more shadows onto the night-blackened woods.

He looked to his right and saw another figure. It was Cyclops, standing about twenty yards away. He could tell from the distinctive cut of his punked-up hair.

Even when he wasn't in costume, Cyclops was a fright. He'd earned his nickname because he was overly fond of removing the glass eye that replaced the eye he'd lost in a gangboy brawl. Ever since then, he'd been revenging himself on the man who did it, figuring that out of the dozen or so he'd killed, one of them might have been the culprit.

Cyclops was a man who liked to shoot. They all did, he thought. Even the girl, Gwen McCardle. She'd been the killing kind long before Derek Martin recruited her. Even if it wasn't for Shock Troupe, there would be blood on her hands.

But since she was in the troupe, she had no choice but to perform according to Derek Martin's scenario. If the script said kill, you didn't ask why. Instead of asking what the motivation was, you just pulled the trigger. The motivation was that if you didn't, someone would pull the trigger on you.

Whitehouse looked around for Martin. He couldn't see any sign of him, but that was no great surprise. Martin was fond of skulking about. He was fully in his element in a place like this. Lying hidden somewhere, waiting to pounce, waiting to shock.

There was a chill in the air. The wind had picked up since they'd first come out. Hissing. Shushing. Feeling vulnerable all of a sudden, Whitehouse headed for the stack of weapons he'd cached.

He crouched down by a pile of brush and pushed aside the branches, feeling around on the damp earth for the canvas satchel.

It was gone!

His fingers became claws as he dug into the dirt frantically.

Ahhh. He let out a heartfelt sigh. He had found the cache. His heart jumped back down from his throat as he drew the satchel toward him.

It felt lighter. He tore at it, then stared in surprise. What the hell?

There was only one Sterling SMG in the satchel. He held it tightly as though it was a lost heirloom recovered after twenty years of searching.

Had one of the others felt the same sense of unease as he did, Whitehouse wondered, and taken it out? No. It didn't feel right.

Maybe he should call out for Martin.

Forget it, he told himself. That would give him away. If there was a hostile force in the area, he didn't want to give away his position.

Then the darkness moved.

A shape separated itself from the darkness. For a brief moment, the stuntman saw moonlight shining on glistening black eyes. A face surrounded by a splintery halo of brush moved in on him.

It was a wild man, the branches looking like a war bonnet, Whitehouse thought. An Indian was on the warpath....

Whitehouse reacted by instinct. He opened up with the Sterling SMG. But nothing happened. There was a blunted metallic sound. It was jammed. Somebody had jammed his machine gun.

''No—''

The shout that was about to emerge was hammered silent by a backfist. Whitehouse tumbled back from the massive blow, thrashing through the woods head over heels. He snatched at his knife, but suddenly his hand was numb.

The Indian's foot had smashed into his wrist, shattering it like chicken bones. Then the foot flicked out again. This time Whitehouse saw the blow coming, just before it caved in his skull.

The woods lit up then.

Alerted by Whitehouse's short-lived cry, Derek Martin emerged from the woods. He squeezed off several 7.65 mm rounds from his Waltern XL47E automatic pistol. The shots flamed toward the spot where he'd seen Whitehouse fall.

A scythe of Heckler & Koch automatic fire whipped through the woods as the SOBs unloaded on Shock Troupe. The MP5 SMGs blew off thirty-round clips at eight hundred rounds per minute, whapping into the forest and into the black-clad but outclassed ambushers.

Martin heard screams as his men fell piecemeal. After that he heard something worse. He heard silence, a silence broken only by quick rustling sounds through the brush. Then another fusillade of automatic fire came his way.

Martin dropped to the ground and rolled, unholstering his Ingram M10 machine pistol and spraying wildly in a semicircle in front of him.

It didn't matter that some of his own people might be there. All that mattered was that he clear a path and get free. Actors could perish. It was the director who had to survive.

He slapped another clip into the Ingram and moved into the woods.

BARRABAS STOOD like a sentinel at the edge of the brush. He looked just like the brush in fact, covered by a cape of tendrils and twigs, the makeshift camouflage adding to his gillie suit.

He heard the approach of rapid footsteps, though it was plain that some care was taken to subdue the sounds.

He quieted his breath, exhaling in cadence with the wind whipping through the trees.

The SOBs had herded the would-be assassins toward the peak of the ridge. The Shock Troupers had been so busy envisioning how their quarry would arrive in a few days that they hadn't noticed the "scarecrows" moving through the forest.

The footsteps grew louder. It couldn't be one of his men, he thought. But he wouldn't know for sure until the man was practically right on him. Then the footsteps sounded jerky, panicked.

A split second later they were even more panicked, when Barrabas stepped forward and broadsided him, knocking him off his feet.

The Shock Trouper tumbled to the ground, swinging his head to the right at the same time as he swung his Uzi submachine gun.

But the "scarecrow" was moving through the air. One hand batted away the Uzi as it thudded a 9 mm burst into the ground, kicking up a fountain of dirt and shattered shale.

Barrabas's right hand streaked forward like a launched rocket, clacking the man's jaw together with two extended knuckles.

Blood and cracked teeth sprayed from his mouth. His head twisted to the side and stopped dead.

Barrabas got to his feet. He barely had time to realize that the faint blur of movement was the Uzi turning his way.

He reached through sheer reflex and dropped like a puppet that had its strings cut, digging his heels in the ground and pushing off at the same moment. Even as he was falling backward he drew his Browning Hi-Power and squeezed off a round that thwacked the man in the chest.

The Uzi fired overhead.

Barrabas sat straight up and fired again, a coup shot that cored the man's head and kept him down for good.

DEREK MARTIN RAN for his life, stopping only when a flare whumped into the sky and rained light down onto the woods.

He stopped and looked around him.

Scarecrows came to life. They stepped from the woods and poured automatic fire into the path his ambushed Shock Troupers were taking.

The scarecrows were visible only for split seconds. They would fire, then move on to stop and fire again.

"Beautiful," Martin whispered. "Bloody fucking beautiful." Like a scene from one of his movies, he thought. A hellish scene lit by Lucifer himself.

Several flares floated earthward, dropping more shimmering light onto the darkness. But the destructive beauty of the scene lost its fascination as several submachine rounds zipped past his head.

Martin tried to see how many there were. How many men had taken his troupe out?

A woman! There was a woman with them, firing and moving quicker than any of the Shock Troupers.

He gave up. He couldn't count them.

Especially when he wasn't looking back. His instinct for survival was leading him into the wilderness, his narrow axlike face slashing through the branches, heedless of the bloody trails they scored across his face.

THE MOOR WAS THE SITE of many prehistoric hill forts and cairns for the dead.

Archaeologists had tried in vain to reconstruct the battles the ancient warriors fought here, just like they would try in vain to reconstruct tonight's covert battle that had seeded the ground with flesh and blood.

Soldiers and mystics had fought here a millenium ago. Soldiers like the five men and one woman who now scoured the field taking a body count and looking for the leader of Shock Troupe.

But Derek Martin wasn't there. Somehow he'd made it through. Perhaps he and a few other troupers had survived the battle.

Barrabas stood by the shattered remnants of the terrorists. One of them was clutching a camera in one hand, a weapon in the other.

"Show's over, pal" Barrabas said.

Shock Troupe had made their mistake by considering themselves a real army, rather than just a bunch of bloody assassins.

Now that they'd run into the Soldiers of Barrabas they knew the difference between skilled soldiers and ruthless murderers.

They were literally worlds apart.

AS SOON AS THE SOBs drove back to the safehouse on the shore, Barrabas called Jessup to send a clean-up crew to the kill zone.

"What about Martin?" Jessup questioned.

"He got away for now," Barrabas said. "He could be anywhere at the moment—on a yacht that sailed down from Bristol for him, or he could still be on foot. We've searched the entire area and he's gone. *If* in fact, Martin was the one running the show after all."

"Oh, it was him, all right," Jessup replied. "Brendan Laird just forwarded me a copy of a tape made by Thomas Crowell. The INS crusader committed suicide. But before he went out, Crowell made a tape on which he confessed his part in Shock Troupe and fingered Martin as the man who was controlling him and a few other people in the media."

"Is this public yet?" Barrabas asked.

"No. So far the Brits are keeping a lid on the tape."

"That means Martin doesn't know if he's been exposed yet," Barrabas said. "So when his world is crashing around him, where will he go?" Barrabas asked.

"Home," Jessup answered.

"Right. He's thinking that either he'll be safe for now and no one suspects him. Or else he'll be bringing his people for a last-ditch effort. Another option is to grab weapons, money, and run."

"I'm with you," Jessup said. "*If* he comes home. Remember, the crazy are different from you and me."

True, Barrabas thought. But then, remembering some of the missions that Jessup had sent the SOBs on, he realized that crazy was a matter of degree.

"It's the only game we've got," Barrabas said. "If Martin shows, I've arranged a welcome-home party. If not, we'll track him down. But for now, get in touch with Laird with instructions to bring in the wrecking crew we discussed."

"What've you got planned?" Jessup asked.

"We're going to make a movie," Barrabas answered.

19

A triad of USAF PAVE LOW III helicopters flew over the southern England terrain, carrying a cargo of SOBs.

Comprising half of the 21st Special Operations Squadron based at RAF Woodbridge in Suffolk, the three helicopters employed terrain-following radar and computer-generated mapping to fly fast and low over the countryside.

Officially a part of NATO, the squadron's anti-terrorist role called for it to deploy special operations forces anywhere in Europe.

This one was right in their backyard.

Barrabas had arranged for the unit to ferry the SOBs from the Bristol area to their next battlefield.

The coming confrontation was at King's Glen, where Brendan Laird already had a welcoming committee in place. The SAS crew had laid low while Derek Martin and his refugees from the firefight on the moors straggled back to the King's Glen manor in a trickle of cars.

After Shock Troupe had amassed their forces at the manor, Laird ordered a containment action.

SAS crews blockaded the roads leading to the manor, posting signs that claimed a film was in progress. Shooting on location was nothing unusual for the area. Even in the middle of a dark morning filming wasn't totally unheard of.

Directors like Derek Martin had a reputation of going to great lengths to get the perfect shot, and he was known far and wide as an eccentric.

World War III could have gone off at the manor and the distant neighbors would have complained that the greedy filmmaker was at it again with his explosions and loud special effects.

After the area was sealed off, the SAS breach-and-entry team waited for the PAVE III helos to arrive.

When the helos swooped in fast, coming in without lights, the SAS technical team neutralized the surveillance monitors on the perimeter of the manor.

Brendan Laird and his assault team moved forward.

They stormed the house as the drone of the helicopters grew louder. Using shaped charges and hammers, Laird's crew smashed through the reinforced doors, while the helos hovered above the roof, dropping several rope ladders at once.

The SOBs dropped from the helicopters onto the gabled roof at the same time as the SAS raised hell below. Submachine gun fire, flash-bang grenades and shaped charges blasted several new entryways into the manor.

Claude Hayes and Lee Hatton gained access through upper-floor balconies, then set about making as much noise as the SAS team, throwing smoke and stun grenades in front of them as they searched the top floor.

Barrabas and O'Toole rappeled down the front side of the building while Billy Two and Nanos scaled down the back. Using a rapid-drop descent, Barrabas knifed down to the middle floor.

Planting his feet solidly on the side of the building, he swung out in a wide pendulum, then came in feet first, crashing through the latticed windows.

Glass shards skidded over his flak jacket as he soared into the room, scanning the surroundings with the harnessed MP5 SMG coiled in his right arm.

There was no resistance.

He landed, rolled and moved across the room, ready to fire at an angle through the open doorway. But nothing moved on the floor, nothing except the SOBs as they crashed their way into the manor, sweeping from room to room.

The SAS entry team found no resistance either, quickly moving through the dust and smoke from the explosions they'd used to tear through the doors.

DEREK MARTIN WATCHED the progress of the assault teams on a bank of monitors.

The moment the outside monitors were knocked out and the choppers arrived, he'd summoned the remaining Shock Troupers down to the bottom floor.

Here they would make their stand.

Gwen McCardle leaned over Martin's shoulder to follow the unfolding action above them. It looked like a nightmare come to life.

The men moving so expertly through the hallways wore black commando garb, some of them equipped with respirators that made them look as if they'd dropped in from another planet—or one of Martin's low-budget horror movies. Many of them wore flash hoods that lent them a sinister look.

"They're going to get us if we just wait here," she spoke up finally. Her eyes flickered nervously over the screens as she smoothed her black hair from her face.

She bit her lip, too, Martin noticed. A perfect damsel in distress.

"They're going to kill everybody—" There was a dawning panic in her voice, a certain escalating shrillness. The good times were coming to an end.

"Yes," Martin agreed, as if it were the most natural thing in the world, as if he was looking forward to the threat.

"I have to talk to them," she said as she glanced about wildly.

"This is the best way to play it," he said. "Trust me."

"We're not on a fucking movie set!" she screamed. She pounded his shoulders, pushing him forward onto the console. Then she ran for the door.

Thirty-two rounds of 9 mm ammunition beat her to it, slicing through her body along the way. Bits and pieces of Gwen McCardle splashed a bloody mosaic on the door before she collapsed to the floor, sliding in an ever-growing pool of red.

Martin had emptied the full clip of the Ingram as an inspiration to others.

No one else shared his enthusiasm. Not even Cyclops, the man who'd done some of the best Shock Troupe hits. He was a natural at that, but now he looked discomfitted. As if he had to play a role he wasn't accustomed to.

"Listen...Derek..." Cyclops said, his eyes watching the monitors as the attack teams shot out the surveillance cameras one by one. One instant the screen was showing the commandos firing. Then they'd white out in the next.

"What is it?" Martin said. His voice was irritated, the way it was whenever someone interrupted him when he worked behind the camera. But now he was just part of the audience himself.

"I'd like to play it another way—if that's all right with you..."

Martin allowed for little or no improvisation, unless the trouper was particularly gifted. Cyclops was considered one of the select.

"Before they get down to this level, let me wait for them in the hall outside," Cyclops said. "If I get out there now, I might be able to take the first group out—and then we come out on top instead of getting snuffed down here."

"Give it your best," Martin said. "Make us all proud..."

Cyclops nodded. He picked up a Sterling submachine gun, and cast just one backward glance as he headed for the door of the war room.

"Open the door for him," Martin said.

There were five other people in the room. All of them headed for the door to unlock it for Cyclops.

Martin laughed. "All thinking like one entity," he said. "Now that's a real troupe. That's the way it should be. Each actor knowing just what the other is thinking."

The sight of them clustered around the doorway in fear sickened him. They would ruin the moment. "Go out with him if you want,'' he said. ''Go out and take your last bow.''

Derek Martin let the herd free. He locked the door behind them, then sat back down at the command center, and on the monitor he watched the last performance of Shock Troupe.

Cyclops was true to his word. He tried to find a way out for them all. At the first bend in the corridor he nearly cut an SAS commando in two with a quick burst of his Sterling. But he only managed to wound a second man who fired three pistol shots into Cyclops. One in the head, one in the heart, and one in the stomach.

It was perfect cinema.

So perfect that Martin didn't even need to film it, he just had to experience it. Long ago he'd decided there was no sense in filming the inevitable hit when it came. The damned government would never show the film.

Besides, this way he could fully enjoy the scene he had created. There was no need of cameras. Just his eyes alone could photograph the scene forever.

The corridor outside the War Room filled with bodies. Shock Troupe bodies. They were cut down most professionally while they fired sporadically at the commandos, using up the ammunition in futile bursts.

Martin was down to one monitor now.

A white-haired man appeared on the screen. Clearly it was the leader of the assault force. He walked through the smoke, stepping over the bodies.

The mercenary looked up then. Almost as if he were looking Martin right in the eye, he lifted his SMG and strafed the camera.

As the last monitor whited out, Martin shut down the board. He loaded another clip into the Ingram M10. Then he pushed his wheeled chair away from the console, giving him a clear shot at the doorway.

He'd had the event scripted for years. The way it would be. The way he would go out.

They would smash through the doors. The leader would burst in—and Martin would burst *him*. Then the rest of the commandos would gun the director down. The last scenario of Derek Martin would come to an end.

"Beautiful," he thought. "Bloody fucking beautiful." He pictured it in his head. *Gunfight at the O K Corral.* Gunfight at King's Glen.

But the door didn't burst in.

He waited. He felt blind without the monitors to watch everything that was going on outside the War Room. But he forced himself to stay silent and wait.

Then he heard a *thunk*. It came not from the door but from the wall beside it.

Thunk! As he strained his ears to identify the sound, it was repeated again. It was followed by a low hissing sound. He understood. Gas. They were using gas on him.

Tear gas filtered into the room. Jets of it poured from all sides of the door. His eyes began to water. His throat started to close.

"No!" he shouted. "Not like thisssss!" He sputtered some more, but compelled by the growing distress, he had no choice. He stumbled toward the door. Slowly he opened it and stepped into the hallway, wiping his eyes with the back of his shirtsleeve.

In his right hand was the Ingram M10. "It's not in the script," he wailed, staggering out.

"It's your call," Barrabas said.

Martin shook his head from left to right, straining to see the mercenary. He raised the Ingram.

Barrabas zipped him with a three-round burst that knocked him back through the open door.

Martin staggered to the console, the Ingram still in his hand. He collapsed onto his chair, and saw Nile Barrabas standing at the end of the haze.

It wasn't right. His opponent was supposed to die first—a last satisfaction. Then Martin could die. . . .

He pitched forward onto the console. The room was spinning around. In his movies this was the control center, the place where the monsters were slain.

One last effort was needed. He pulled the trigger of the Ingram, and it fired wildly.

Barrabas put an end to the distorted celluloid dreams with a final 9 mm burst that spun Martin off his chair onto the floor.

The white-haired slayer stepped back from the fog of cordite and gas that spilled from the room as the stillness of death settled over Derek Martin.

Barrabas turned at the sound of footsteps behind him as the SOBs trooped down the hallway, looking toward the open door.

O'Toole was the first to get there. He cast an inquiring glance at the interior of the bizarre command center.

"How is it?" he demanded.

"It's a wrap, people," Barrabas said. "Let's get going."

In Bolan's never-ending war against organized crime, the hunter has become the hunted. But the battle is only beginning.

DON PENDLETON's

MACK BOLAN

Framed for murder and wanted by both sides of the law, Bolan escapes into the icy German underground to stalk a Mafia-protected drug baron.

TAKE 'EM NOW

FOLDING SUNGLASSES
FROM GOLD EAGLE

Mean up your act with these tough, street-smart
shades. Practical, too, because they fold 3 times
into a handy, zip-up polyurethane pouch that fits
neatly into your pocket. Rugged metal frame.
Scratch-resistant acrylic lenses. Best of all, they
can be yours for only $6.99.

MAIL YOUR ORDER TODAY.

Send your name, address, and zip code, along with a check or
money order for just $6.99 + .75¢ for postage and handling (for a
total of $7.74) payable to Gold
Eagle Reader Service.
(New York and Iowa
residents please add
applicable sales tax.)

Remove from pouch...

unfold once...

GOLD EAGLE
Gold Eagle Reader Service
901 Fuhrmann Blvd.
P.O. Box 1396
Buffalo, N.Y. 14240-1396

unfold twice...

and they're ready to wear.

GES-1A

Offer not available in Canada.

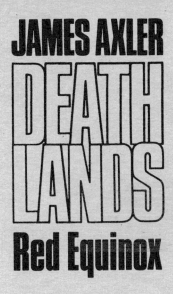

Nile Barrabas's most daring mission is about to begin . . .

THE BARRABAS BLITZ

JACK HILD

An explosive situation is turned over to a crack commando squad led by Nile Barrabas when a fanatical organization jeopardizes the NATO alliance by fueling public unrest and implicating the United States and Russia in a series of chemical spills.
